DOM DADDY

MASTER OF KINK

SAM MARIE

DOM DADDY

MASTER OF KINK

Dom Daddy by Sam Marie

Published by Sam Marie

www.authorsammarie.com

Cover by Sam Marie

ISBN: 979-8-9893802-5-1 (ebook)

ISBN: 979-8-9893802-4-4 (paperback)

Printed in the USA

First Edition

*To my younger self and anyone who needs this reminder,
Not all love is equal, but the love you give yourself is unparalleled.
Give it in abundance, in every form, and at every moment. Do not be
ashamed to embrace the good, the bad, and the in-between. Because life
is what you make it. If you only get one—make it fucking awesome!*

Trigger and Content Warnings

Be advised the following stories may contain triggering terms, situations, and themes that may cause disturbing or unexpected emotions. Please understand this is a work of fiction and may not depict the exact dynamic of a BDSM relationship or realistic events. This is what I call a reverse harem, non-traditional happily ever after—it's all about the female main character and her happily ever after (which may not be the stereotypical monogamous relationship). I advise reading this book with an open mind about relationships and expectations. Below are the themes, kinks, and other potentially triggering content:

online dating, mutual masturbation, polyamory, non-monogamous, sexting, toys, unprotected sex, foreign objects used as toys, public masturbation, degradation, edging, power play, slapping, spitting, marking, bukkake/facial, double penetration, threesome, creampie, bondage, preconceived manipulation/control, public fornication, food play, oral, slave play, vaginal and anal fingering, voyeurism, whipping, nipple and labia clamps, queening, tribbing, lesbian, sawhorse, pinwheel, restraints, plugs, Eiffel tower, aftercare, collar, leash, asphyxiation, squirting, group play, animal role-play/pet play, cage, breeding, temperature play

Contents

Serious Inquiries Only

It's been five months since I last got laid, and it wasn't anything special. In fact, I actively try to forget how terrible it was, and lately, my vibrator simply isn't cutting it. Even my favorite porn star doesn't excite me anymore. I need a release—a no-strings-attached, raunchy release.

This is why I find myself setting up a profile on the sketchiest dating apps available.

Is it wise to seek out a man who just wants to hook up? Probably not. Does it hurt to look? Definitely not. Does it hurt to talk to them and see what they have to offer? Also, probably not. It's harmless entertainment, after all.

I haven't met anyone in person. At least, not yet. I question whether I actually would meet up with a total stranger. Especially with the expectation and sole purpose of hooking up. What would we talk about? Would we just get straight to fucking?

The last time I was on these dating sites was in college so I'm completely out of my realm. The idea of meeting up with someone for sex is both exciting and scary. Honestly, I don't know if I'll follow through with a meetup, but swiping left and right on people's profiles is helping curve my horniness, and it isn't putting me in danger. I'm safe behind the glass screen, for now.

Since I'm looking for sex with no emotional connection, I press the like button on every hot guy. I don't expect many to match me back, but I hope there are at least a few good contenders.

It takes time for matches to show up, and just when I think no one will match me this evening, I see a photo of a stylishly dressed man with an emoji covering his face.

His profile description reads: *Dom looking for a sub. In an open relationship but like to keep things discreet. Serious inquiries only.*

This is one of the sketchier dating apps, but this is also the first profile I've come across with a description that matches precisely what I'm looking for. The fact that the man hides his face is a major red flag—he's probably a catfish—but I'll take the risk if it means getting exactly what I want.

I swipe right, and we immediately match. My heart flutters excitedly. I sincerely hope he's not a catfish. He's got great shoulders, and his style makes me envious. If he has the face to match and the conversation is spicy, I'll be in literal orgasmic heaven.

However, a thread of fear starts to wind around my racing heart as I wonder if he'll like me once we start chatting. I don't know much about the dom–sub culture, but I've seen my fair share of porn, and it's something I wouldn't mind trying. If the mystery man doesn't think my lack of experience is unattractive, this may be my chance for some life-changing sex.

Steeling my nerves, I send the man named Jones a message.

Hi!

Hey, Sexy! What are you doing right now?

> Um… Just scrolling through the app. Haha

> Do you want to meet and do something more fun?

I have a faint idea of what something *more fun* entails, but the rational woman in me needs to get to know this guy a little bit before I meet him in person. He could be a serial killer, for all I know. Plus, I need details.

It's been a long time since I have touched or been touched. I need to know I'll be safe. I need to know how far this "dom" thing goes and what he plans to do to me. However, my thirsty lady parts don't seem to care much about safety right now as they pulse with excitement. My fingers shake as I type my response.

> Like what?

> I don't like to beat around the bush, metaphorically speaking, of course. I'll beat your bush if you have one. ;) I'm looking for someone to play with. Are you into that?

> Play with…sexually?

> That's right, Kitten. I'm just looking for a sub who knows how to follow orders and wants to come harder than she's ever come before.

His messages make my pussy throb insistently. This is the perfect no-strings-attached scenario I'm looking for.

A man who just wants to play, who just wants to focus on the pleasure. I need that.

But I still don't know who he is or how this works. His messages seem too good to be true—like he's reading my mind.

> What does a sub do?

> I can show you, but essentially, you let me control you. It's all pleasurable—I promise. I want you to be comfortable. If something doesn't feel right, all you have to do is tell me to stop. We can talk about it more when we meet.

> But I haven't even seen your face. How do I know it's safe?

Laying all my cards on the table might not be the smartest move. A serial killer will do everything possible to make me feel safe, and now he knows I'm suspicious. But my vagina is begging me to keep this conversation going because if it is real, this might be all I need to shove my sexual repression aside.

> We can chat over video if that makes you feel better. Plus, we can meet somewhere public. I want you to feel safe.

> But let me get one thing straight: I'm not looking to wine and dine someone. I have a relationship. While I might treat you to lingerie and late-night cocktails, there will always be the promise of something sexual involved when we meet.

He's being totally transparent about his desires, which leads me to trust him more. I can't explain the feeling; maybe it's intuition, but I believe he's being honest.

> Your profile says you're in an open relationship, so I assumed it wouldn't be anything more…

> Good. I'm glad we are on the same page. This is still mutually beneficial, but only in terms of sexual satisfaction.

Safety is still on the back of my mind. The fear that stems from traumatic past experiences is forever present.

Yet, my pussy begs me to accept his video chat proposal. Because if I'm being honest, taking the risk to meet in person will require a lot of trust, or for him to be so hot I can't say no, and I have yet to see his face.

I'm safe behind a screen; a video call will give me time to decide. I'll get to see if he's real and get a better idea of how much further I'm willing to go with him.

> I'd feel better if we video chat first, like you suggested.

> No problem. But…I want you playing with your pussy when you answer the phone. I do things one way—my way. This will give you an idea of how good I'll make you feel and prove to me how good a sub you can be. Understand, Kitten?

My lower lips moisten, imagining being on the phone with a strange man and touching myself in front of him.

Good god, I'm ridiculously horny.

I run out of the living room, into my bedroom, lock the door, and get under the covers of my bed. Reaching over, I grab my hot pink vibrator from the bedside drawer, set it beside me, and slip my fingers under the hemline of my pants while I type a response to Jones.

> When would you like to chat?

> Now.

My heart stops.

This is actually happening.

My fingers are already rotating small circles around the bundle of nerves at the peak of my vagina, but nothing can prepare me for this. A pulsing ache beats as fast as my heart between my legs, pumping arousal to the area between my thighs and readying me for my call with Jones.

> Okay.

Jones calls me immediately using the video chat function on the dating app. I hit the answer button and hold the camera at the most flattering angle possible when lying against a pillow. It's not the best, but it will have to do.

When the screen lights up, connecting our video call, Jones' face greets me, and I am far from disappointed. I already knew he had a hot body, but his face is all sharp angles and smooth skin with dark, angry brows. He is the epitome of what I imagine a dom should look like. It's going to be very hard for me to resist this man. I gulp as dryness builds in my throat.

"Hi, Kitten." He purrs a greeting like it's a sensual promise.

My knees are weak. If I were standing, I'd soon be on the ground, kneeling before him.

"Hi," I respond shyly. I don't know how to do this. My fingers pause their circling, but my heart races faster as I study every inch of him and wait for the dom to take the lead. If this were a sink-or-swim situation, I'd be sinking. Insecurity racks my body.

"Are you playing with your pussy like Daddy told you to do?"

Oh fuck. He's jumping straight into it. I don't know what else to do except exactly what he tells me. I follow his lead like a puppy on a leash. "Yes," I say, glancing down to where my fingers hesitantly start circling again under the covers.

"Good girl. Tell me, what will it take to get you to meet me, Kitten?" he asks while licking his thin lips. They're severe and punishing to behold.

"I don't know…" I say, still rubbing circles around my clit while my mind races disbelievingly at the fact that I'm actually masturbating while video chatting with a stranger.

"Do you want Daddy to show you how he'll make you feel?"

"How are you going to do that?" I ask curiously, sliding a finger between my lower lips and feeling the wetness soaking me down there.

"Can you take orders, Kitten?"

"Yes."

"Good. Show Daddy you're doing what he said," he demands. His voice is stoic and uncompromising.

"Hold on," I breathe heavily, setting the phone down and tugging my pants and underwear off under the covers.

I toss the clothes to the side and pull the blanket down. The cold bedroom air kisses my wet skin, forcing me to shiver and my nipples to tighten under my camisole. I masturbate often, but I've never responded as quickly as this.

Turning the camera around, I show Jones what he asked to see. I suck in a breath, waiting for him to be disappointed by my body. I'm nothing special. On a good day, my thighs don't chafe, and right now, my entire lower body, glistening folds and fingers are on full display.

"That's a very pretty pussy," Jones says huskily. "Get the camera closer. I want to see your cunt pulsing."

My stomach clenches at his vulgar words. My flaws do not deter him, if he sees them at all. So I follow his command, holding the camera closer to my pussy, while keeping the screen turned so I can see his facial expressions.

"Now spread your lips and open up for Daddy."

Again, I do as he commands, spreading my lower lips for him and revealing every crevice of my vagina. My entry contracts and expands with the quick beat of my heart.

"So beautiful. Put a finger inside your cunt, Kitten," he demands, and I do.

A quiet moan escapes on my breath as I watch Jones's lips part before he bites his bottom lip aggressively. He likes watching me, and I like him watching me even more. I pump my finger in and out of my sex. The slick sound of my arousal only increases my desire.

"Stop," Jones growls.

I pause my movements. My breathing hitches as I wait for his next command. I need it like my life depends on it. I hang on to his every word.

"Do you have a mirror?" he asks.

"Yes," I say. My fingers shake as I itch to give my pussy what it craves.

"Stand in front of the mirror and take your clothes off."

I want to groan from the frustration stopping causes me, but Jones knows what he's doing, and I trust that he'll bring me to orgasm, so I turn the camera around and stand in front of my closet mirror, waiting for his directions.

"Take off your clothes."

With only my camisole remaining, I pass the camera between my hands as I remove my top. I stand butt-ass naked in front of the mirror with my heavy breasts falling free. Jones's eyes roam my body, intently studying me. He takes his time absorbing every inch of me. Insecurity threatens to take over, to end this call, but Jones says, "Such a beautiful body, Kitten. Those tits are fucking amazing. Rub your tits for Daddy."

I grab my breast with one hand and massage it, giving Daddy a full view of my luscious mounds. They're my favorite body part.

"Pinch your nipple."

I roll my nipple between my thumb and forefinger, causing my pussy to clench harder from its lack of attention. Nothing but air touches me there.

"Harder. Daddy will pinch that nipple much harder, so show me what you can handle, Kitten."

Fuck. His words will be my undoing. My body leaks its desire down my inner thigh. I hear it dripping onto the floor below me as I pinch my nipple to nearly unbearable pain levels and have to bite my lip to silence the moan of pleasure that accompanies it.

"Is that a vibrator behind you?" he asks.

"Yes," I say, panting and squirming, hoping he'll ask me to use it next.

"Get the vibrator. Set up your phone so you can use both hands, and I can see your body. Daddy is going to make you come so you know why you need to meet him."

Yes. I want to come. I need to come.

I scramble to the bed, grab the vibrator, and set up the phone so Jones can see my front and some of my back in the mirror behind me. He smiles unabashedly when I'm done setting up everything for his viewing pleasure. He's proud of me.

"Good girl. Very good. Do you want to see what this does to me, Kitten?"

Jones turns his camera around. He's sitting in the driver's seat of his car, and I can see the massive bulge in the front of his dress slacks. His agile fingers unbutton and unzip the slacks. His cock pops out, unbound by underwear. I whimper at the sight of it. When his fingers wrap around the base of his cock, his girth becomes more apparent. My pussy clenches as if I can feel him inside me.

"You like that?" he asks.

"Yes. Yes, Daddy," I say, licking my lips and imagining his fat cock inside me—inside every part of me. I seriously need to get laid.

"Put the dildo inside your pussy, Kitten. Pretend it's Daddy's cock fucking that tight cunt."

Jones keeps his camera on his cock. Jacking himself off while I take the vibrator and rub it across my pussy lips, lubricating it for entry.

"Yes, Kitten. Put it inside nice and slow."

I do as he instructs, inserting the vibrator slowly. My body feels every inch and groove of it enter me. I watch Jones pump his cock while the vibrator enters me, and my entire body heats ten degrees as I imagine it's Daddy's cock going inside me.

"Now take it out and suck your juices off of it."

"Yes, Daddy," I preen, happy to comply and make a show of it. Bringing the pink dildo to my lips, Jones switches his camera to his face so I can watch his reaction as I lick up the base of the pussy juice-soaked dildo and then suck the entire thing into my mouth. I swirl my tongue around the tip, and Jones groans as he adjusts himself.

"You are so fucking sexy, Kitten. Daddy is pleased with you. Do you want to come now?"

I shake my head enthusiastically, showing him just how much I want to come. Need to come. And how much I want to please him.

"Turn it on and put it back inside your pussy. I want you to thrust it inside your cunt every time I pump my cock."

Following his directions, I thrust the dildo inside my needy cunt and turn on the vibration. The sudden movement forces my walls to clench, and the feeling intensifies as my muscles clamp around it.

"Not yet, Kitten," Jones purrs sweetly as he turns his camera to face his dick again.

With each stroke of his cock, I withdraw and insert the vibrating dildo. Jones increases the pace of his hand, stroking his cock faster as precum beads at the tip of his dick. My mouth waters shamelessly, wanting to lick it off, but the camera separates us, which only fuels that desperate need into the speed of my hand.

"Touch your clit with your other hand," he groans, pushing his hips up as his hand works on his thick cock.

With one hand pushing the dildo into my pussy and the other working my clit, I pick up a steady rhythm that leaves my body shaking, tightening, and squirming. I'm so close.

"Watch Daddy's cock, Kitten. When I come, you come," Jones says. His voice is laced with a threatening edge that tells me I better come, or he'll be delivering punishment. "Say *yes, Daddy*."

"Yes, Daddy," I pant, moving my fingers faster.

"Are you going to meet with Daddy and let him show you how much better he can make you feel than that shitty little vibrator?" he asks, pumping his cock even faster.

"Yes, Daddy," I respond, matching my pace with his. I throw all caution to the wind, hanging on his every word for my release. When he says come, I'm going to explode.

"Are you going to be a good little girl and let Daddy have his way with you?"

"Yes, Daddy."

"You're a good girl. Aren't you, Kitten? You'll do exactly as Daddy says, even when I take your ass."

My entire body shudders, sucking in the vibrator and refusing to release it as the vibrations shoot up my center, and I scream, "Yes, Daddy."

"Come," he says.

Jones's cum spurts up in the air and lands on his cock, sliding down his fingers as he pumps out his release. My orgasm slams into like a wall. Cum rolls down the vibrator onto my fingers as I tremble through the waves of my release.

When the orgasm lulls, I switch off the vibrator before my sensitive bud re-energizes and begs for round two. Daddy hasn't said I can have another.

"Very good, Kitten. Now, was that good, or do you need another one?" Jones asks, wiping the cum off his cock with a napkin.

He could care less that I'm watching him clean up in his car. He's so effortlessly sexy and confident. My fingers unconsciously slide between my thighs, and I drag a finger through the wet, sticky cum. In response to his question, I bring the cum-soaked fingers to my lips and suck on it.

Jones flips the camera around to show me his pleased face. "Very good, Kitten. I'm dropping you a pin. Meet me there in one hour. Wear a tight black dress and no underwear."

I nod my head and say, "Yes, Daddy."

Patio Punishment

J ones dropped me a pin to a fancy bar in West Hollywood, but I bailed. He understood my hesitancy, and we talked more so that I would feel comfortable meeting in person.

Finally, he convinced me to meet him for drinks at a local dive bar down the road from my apartment. It's a low-key vibe, which makes me feel like the expectations will also be low-key. Although, I'm doubting anything with this man will be low-key. The impression the orgasm he gave me was…earth-shattering.

He says he wants me to feel safe, and meeting in a public place where I can vet him as a normal human being, not a serial killer, is the best way to do that. To his credit, he's also driving across the city to meet me. I have a sneaking suspicion it has more to do with avoiding a run-in with people he knows because, come to find out, he's not just in an open relationship; he's married.

His wife knows he likes doing freaky stuff, so she fully supports him messing around with other women. Or so he says. I hope this isn't a complete lie, and I'm actively participating in a cheating scandal. But I'm desperate for a non-committal release, and this man made me come so hard during our video call two days ago.

Every time I masturbate, I think about that moment. Eventually, I concluded that I needed to meet him in person. The idea of a strange man touching my body is nerve-racking, but it's also exciting and makes me wet from the mere thought of it, especially from Jones.

I walk through the door of the dive bar, wave at the bartender, and head to the back patio at the far end of the small joint.

Worry fills my gut as each step brings me closer to the real him. Meeting in person takes me past the safety net of my phone. The anticipation has me in knots. I don't know what to expect. I don't know how I'll feel. But there's no turning back from here. He suggested we meet in the parking lot, but I was purposely running late. Truthfully, I was questioning whether to bail.

Jones warned me that my delay would only make him want me more and that he doesn't appreciate tardiness. A man this incessant is a red flag, but it also makes my knees weak from his sensual arrogance.

He knows what he wants, and he takes it. Repercussions be damned. I'm sure there's some punishment involved on my end. Yet, even that feels like a promise I can't wait to cash in on.

As I push through the patio door, I glimpse Jones in person for the first time. He's even more handsome than on video. The sharp lines of his face are complimented by subtle lines that show his age. His dark hair is cut short on the sides and longer on top. A five o'clock shadow lines his jaw despite the early hour. As if I expected anything less of a man who exudes power and control, he's in what most people consider a suit. His outfit is effortlessly sophisticated and pairs dangerously with the timeless features of his face. I'd bet this is Jones's daily attire, though.

The way he carelessly leans back against an old iron chair with an ankle propped on his knee tells me dirt isn't even a thought. He probably has countless suits and gets them dry-cleaned after every wear. But in keeping up his humbling, casual appearance, Jones sits with a smartphone in one hand and a beer in the other—just like any man having a cheap drink after work.

I take slow steps toward him, setting down my feet softly as if being loud will make this situation more real.

He reminds me of a lion—confident and relaxed, but you know he's ready to pounce at any moment. His perfection makes my breath hitch. He's like sex-walking. The air seems to change around him, running away as if to avoid competing for space. I struggle to understand why he's interested in someone like *me*.

"Kitten," he coos, looking up at me as I sit in the only other chair at the table, which is coincidentally directly beside his.

I turn to speak to him and want to say something quirky or witty, but all I can get out is a strangled garble of words. "Hi," I say.

"Are you nervous?" he asks, setting his beer down and turning to face me with a smirk that makes my heart jerk.

Our knees brush slightly, and I resist the urge to lean away. This man wants to touch me in far more intimate places than this. I won't be getting anywhere if our knees touching scares me off.

"I'm a little nervous," I admit, feeling a chill grace my forehead.

"I can help ease those nerves. Or would you like to ask me some questions first?" he suggests, sliding a hand over my thigh.

He's clearly undeterred by my nerves or beauty—or lack thereof. I wonder how many times he's done this—met people online and fucked them. Although, I suppose his goal isn't just to get me off. He wants to make me his sub—he told me as much.

At his request, I wore a skirt. He also told me not to wear underwear, but that's too foreign for me, so I kept my panties on. These meaningless requests are part of some bigger dom-sub dynamic I'm unfamiliar with.

I did a little research, and from what I gathered online, these demands are part of a test. He's seeing how well I can follow orders and what my boundaries might be. Some interesting articles mentioned that these tests help the dom weed out dangerous subs who don't know their limits. I guess there is some risk to this relationship when the sub doesn't know their breaking point, and a dom doesn't have limits either. It's still a bit much for me to wrap my head around.

The skin on his hand is mostly soft with small rough callouses against the pads of his fingers as it grazes my thigh. I'm unsure what he does for work, but it definitely doesn't involve hard labor. Although, that isn't what I care about anyway. We aren't here to make an emotional connection. I'm here to get off.

"I don't have any questions," I say, having dismissed any lingering thoughts as soon as I saw him. He's devastating.

"Are you sure about that? Because you insisted we meet somewhere public. Although, I can't say this is very public," he shrugs and leans back in his chair, looking around at the old, dingy, and very empty patio.

He has a point. "I just wanted to see if you were real and how I felt around you, I guess," I mumble my useless explanation.

"Come here," Jones says, motioning to his lap.

I slowly stand and turn to sit in his lap, but he stops me.

"Bend over. Let Daddy see that pussy first. Is it dripping for me yet?" he asks, pushing at my lower back and forcing me to bend over. He hisses when he sees my underwear. "I told you not to wear these."

"But I—" I stutter for an explanation and am rewarded with a firm slap to my ass that makes me jump.

Jones pulls my hips back. "Already disobeying me, Kitten. Sit down, now," he commands.

I perch on his lap, my ass still stinging as he yanks my back into his chest before prying my legs apart with his own. His arm latches around my center, holding my arms underneath his forearm while his other hand roams my inner thigh. His fingers trail a path from my knee to my center.

"What are you doing?" I ask breathlessly, looking around to ensure no one is coming outside to check on us. Jones has me pinned. This strange man touches me like he's known my body for years.

"I'm punishing you," he growls in my ear, then tugs my underwear to the side and slides his fingers through my sex.

A breath rushes out of me from this unfamiliar but savagely personal touch. This is happening so fast, and somehow, I'm already soaked. Something about this man triggers my body's response. It's like his scent is an aphrodisiac, making me want to breed, and my body happily obliges.

Jones rubs his entire hand through my pussy, spreading me apart and massaging my folds. He twiddles the achy bud of nerves between my legs and then lavishly rolls his knuckles across my labia. His hands are massive compared to mine; they touch every part of my throbbing vagina. Massaging, moving, twisting. He makes me yearn for more, even though I know we shouldn't be doing this in public.

A whimper passes through my lips as drool pools at the edge of my mouth. Someone could see us, but my hips roll needily. I couldn't ask him to stop if I wanted to.

"You've been a bad girl, Kitten. You don't deserve to get off," he taunts, moving his fingers in a circle at the peak of my sex. The sloshing sound of my arousal grows dauntingly loud on the quiet patio. "But if you beg Daddy, maybe he'll let you."

The image of me begging, on my knees, and sucking his cock, flits through my dirty mind. I'd love to beg him. Recalling the size of his dick, which I only saw in our first video chat, I feel him against my backside.

He feels even larger than the camera made him look. I swivel my hips on top of his stiff cock below me and relish in the feeling of it hardening even more against my ass. I dismiss the fact that my pussy is on full display for anyone who walks through the patio door.

"I said beg, not tease," Jones growls and slaps my pussy. Hard.

A sharp sting shoots across my wet lips. I squeeze my knees together, but Jones's legs keep mine pried apart.

"Beg," he says, slapping my pussy again.

I stifle a moan as the slap brings a new feeling to my lady parts. The punishment and pain are a new sensation that only teases me more. It's a new and even more exciting feeling that makes my stomach coil in knots of sexual frustration. I need a release.

"Please, Daddy. Please forgive me."

"I should shove this cock into that pretty little cunt of yours and show you why next time you won't want to wear panties."

"Yes," I moan, closing my eyes as his fingers find their place against my pussy once again.

My head feels heavy, the lust fogging my brain. He pinches my clit and rolls it between his fingers, forcing my body to spasm against the erotic touch. Then, he flicks it, and the sharp sting of pain goes directly to my core. My walls tighten against emptiness, and I tremble while Jones holds me down. A release is so close, yet so far. I need it desperately. I need the penetration.

"I won't wear panties ever again, Daddy. I promise," I beg, my voice shaking as his fingers continue their taunting symphony.

"No. You won't. Or I'll do this to you for hours. Bringing you to the brink of orgasm without ever letting you get off," he says firmly, smacking my clit again. "But since this is the first time, I'll give you something you'll never forget, Kitten. You'll be calling me night and day for more. You'll be begging on your knees in no time, just as Daddy likes."

He smacks my clit again.

Everything inside me aches. I feel nauseous from needing an orgasm so badly. "Please, Daddy," I whisper, losing energy to talk as I focus everything on my need to unravel under this man's fingers.

Jones shifts under me, lifting my hips as he unbuckles his pants. In a daze, I let his hands control my body. I look around the small patio and silently thank the gods we're still alone because my loss of control makes me doubt I'd stop this even if someone walked out here.

The tearing of a wrapper catches my attention, and I turn my head to see Jones rolling a condom over his cock. The size of him makes my mouth water. He won't fit. I've never taken a cock so thick.

"Show Daddy how sorry you are," he says, leaning back and letting his cock stand straight up.

My lip trembles. So many thoughts plague my brain, but one rules all others—need. Without another thought, I drop myself onto him, soaking up every inch of him in my achy cunt.

I bite my lip, cursing under my breath to keep my moans of pain from reaching the bartender's ears. Jones's cock shoves into me, but not with ease. He fills me so fully that it feels both good and bad. He's sheathed so tightly that I can't move.

The pain and pleasure make me soaked. Jones pats my ass, signaling for me to move. I have to show him I'm worthy of being fucked, so I lift and drop my hips, fighting through the pain as my body adjusts.

My skirt is the only thing that hides our nasty public act from prying eyes. The curve of his manhood strokes my inner walls and feeds the desire that has been building for not only the short amount of time I've waited to meet Jones but also from months and months of celibacy.

His cock feels like coming home. I swear to myself I'll never abstain again.

I buck my hips on top of him, clenching my walls tighter and moving faster and faster, taking him deeper and deeper as I slam down onto him. My insatiable need burns hot and heavy. It's an unquenchable thirst for a man I know nothing about to get me off harder than I've ever gotten off. A man who I long to prove my worthiness to, if only for another chance to have his cock again.

That's what I want. That's what I need.

"Your cunt is so tight, Kitten. Do you like when Daddy fucks you raw?" he groans, placing his hands on my hips and steadying me so he can thrust himself upward.

"I would, but you aren't fucking me raw," I breathe heavily, stilling as his pelvis pounds into me with unharnessed fury. I'm ready to lose it.

"That's right, but now I am." He lifts me and tears off the condom.

Before I can protest, he thrusts his hips into me. I whimper at the intrusion. It feels so much better raw, and it's not just from no barrier—it's from his claiming. He's taking me and going to fill me up with his cum whether I like it or not. But honestly, I fucking love it. I've thrown all caution to the wind. He sent me a negative STD test results a couple of days ago anyway. And I told him I hadn't had sex in months.

"I'm going to come in you, and then we're going to leave so I can really fuck you. Do you understand me, Kitten? I'm going to take you somewhere, and I won't stop filling that sweet cunt of yours until my cum is dripping down your legs because it can't fit anymore." Daddy growls in my ear as his cock continues punishing me.

His words are like gasoline to a flame, feeding the fire and making me tingle all over.

"Say *yes, Daddy*," he says, increasing his pace and stroking my G-spot with every thrust.

He pounds into me, hitting the part of me that toys and fingers can never reach or touch just right. My arousal, my desire, my fucking pussy is in overdrive. The sensitivity increases with each movement. And when I think I can't handle it any longer, his relentless thrusts push me over the edge.

"Yes, Daddy. Fill me." I explode under his command, bucking against his hips as my juices slide down his cock and shamelessly soil his pants.

Highway Hedonism

"Get in the back," Jones says, pointing to the backseat door of his black Porsche Cayenne.

I do as he says while he tosses my ruined underwear in the street trash can. Jones enters the driver's seat while I buckle myself.

"Where are we going?" I ask, shifting around uncomfortably as my arousal soaks the leather seat under me.

He gives me a look that says he knows exactly what's happening but doesn't address the issue. "To a parking garage. It'll have to do for now."

"Okay..." I say, looking out the window as Jones drives us to an undisclosed location.

I didn't exactly do a proper investigation on him. The ever-apparent possibility that he might be taking me to a parking garage to skin me alive is starting to creep into the rational thought-processing side of my brain.

"Why don't you entertain me while we drive there?" he suggests.

"How should I do that?"

"Take off your clothes," he says as he merges onto the highway.

"But...People might see?" I say as cars fly past us.

"I doubt they're paying attention. Regardless, I told you to get naked, so unless you want to be punished—and I can ensure this punishment won't be as immediately gratifying—you'll do as I say."

"Okay," I say hesitantly, but I can't deny him. I don't know what punishment entails, but I know getting naked will likely lead to a satisfying end. I undress. He motions for me to hand him my clothes, so I do. Jones puts them in the passenger seat beside him and adjusts the rearview mirror to face me.

"Now, play with yourself, Kitten. I want you so ready to come that when I'm finally inside you, you're coming instantly."

Jones's words ignite the flame of desire within me. The promise of being inside me again is enough to make me forget any doubts.

"Okay," I say, beginning to play with myself.

"It's *yes, Daddy*, or *yes, sir* to you. Do you understand?" His hands tighten on the steering wheel. The promise of punishment is evident in the whites of his knuckles.

"Yes, Daddy," I respond obediently. However, part of me is curious about being punished.

"Actually, take this and fuck yourself with it." He tosses an empty plastic bottle at me.

I catch it and hold it up. The rough edges of it make my lower body clench in a new kind of fear. What type of person uses trash as a fuck toy?

"But—" I protest, but Jones cuts me off.

"This is a small punishment for making me wait two days to see you, meeting you at a shitty bar, wearing underwear, and forgetting how to address me. Do you understand what happens when you don't do what Daddy says?" His words are harsh and unyielding.

I gulp down the growing lump in my throat while my pussy quivers. "Yes, Daddy," I say, bowing my head and eyeing the bottle.

"Stick it in," he says with a growl.

I press the lid of the bottle against my entry. The sharp edges of the lid roughly shove into me, but I keep pushing, and once the cap is inside me, the rest of the bottle slides in. However, I'm panting by the time the bottle is half inside me. This entire scenario has my body buzzing with adrenaline.

"Not so bad, huh?" Jones says smugly.

My walls tighten around the smooth sides of the bottle. It glides against my skin. I hide a smile and begin to fuck myself with the bottle, realizing I sort of like this punishment. This is as good, if not better, than a dildo. It's wider but has some give.

Traffic slows, and we pull to a stop on the highway while I beat the plastic bottle into my pussy. I'm still stretched from Jones's cock, and my head is so fuzzy that the action merely lulls me into a deep state of relaxation. The bottle fills me with ease but lacks the firmness of his penis.

As we creep up next to another SUV, I lay flat on the backseat, trying to hide from onlookers, but the seatbelt digs into my side and forces my back to arch off the leather bench. My hand pauses as I debate reaching for my clothes in the front seat to cover myself or unbuckling instead. I want to stay in this post-orgasmic haze forever, but wandering eyes and tedious seat belts are messing with my vibe.

"If you stop, I'll make your punishment public, Kitten," he warns.

"What do you mean?" I ask, slowly moving the bottle as I press myself onto the leather bench, hoping I can't be seen by other vehicles. The seatbelt buckle makes my side cramp, forcing me to stop and try to get comfortable.

"Did I say you could stop?"

"No, Daddy," I say. It comes out as a whine.

"Then continue."

I continue, deciding to unbuckle the seatbelt. With the pain in my side gone, I focus on thrusting the bottle faster and pushing my hips into it as I do so. My heart begins to race. Jones puts his hand down his pants now that traffic is at a complete standstill. My eyes jump from the SUV window next to us to Jones's hand.

"Get on your knees, pussy facing me," he says, turning his head to look at me.

I scramble to my knees on the floorboard, arching my back so my pussy is on display for him and less apparent to anyone looking into the vehicle windows.

"Keep going," he says.

I reach under myself and insert the head of the bottle again.

"Slower."

His words are clipped, but I know what he wants. I pull the bottle in and out of my pussy as slowly as possible; the new speed re-ignites my nerves.

"Play with your clit too," he demands, his hand curving over my backside and spreading my butt cheeks.

To work my clit with my other hand, I press my face against the back seat while both hands are under me, fucking my pussy with a bottle and fondling myself with the other. It's the most uncomfortable position I've ever been in, and yet, the most erotic. I do as he says, moving my hands slowly and feeling a ridiculous amount of wetness between my legs. I can't remember the last time I was this turned on.

"Good girl," he says as he presses a finger against my puckered asshole.

"What are you doing, Daddy?" I ask breathlessly but don't stop. I can't stop. The only thing that might entice me to stop is Jones promising me something more satisfying.

"Don't mind me, Kitten. Fuck—" he curses as traffic begins to move and withdraws his hand.

His hand leaving my body is like drinking the last sip of water in the desert. I need it back. I need to know what that finger inside my backside feels like.

He told me before that he would take my ass, and the anticipation has my sex clamping down on the plastic bottle so hard that it begins to deflate. The change in shape has new grooves massaging my inner walls as I move the bottle in and out. It's rough on the edges, slicing against me, but I love the pain.

The car shifts into movement, rocking my body from side to side, but I keep my knees spread to maintain my balance.

Before I know it, Jones is racing down the highway again, and the pace of my hands increases. I hear Jones tell me something, but I'm lost in pleasure. That coiling, tightening, out-of-body feeling hits me like a ton of bricks, and I'm spewing. My release spurts out of me onto the middle console where Jones's arm rests.

"Kitten," he says harshly, swerving off the highway.

I'm thrown to the floor and still in a daze as Jones pulls to a stop. His door slams before he rounds the car and throws open the back door. The white sleeve of his button-down shirt is soaked in my cum. I struggle to remove the deflated bottle from my pussy, but before I can, Jones is in the back seat, pushing me onto my ass with the bottle still in me.

It sinks impossibly deeper, and I scream as his hand latches around my throat. My breath catches.

"I told you not to come, Kitten."

His hand remains in place, not squeezing but holding. I wait for him to deliver my punishment. Is this it? Is this the moment he fucks me to death?

"You're going to suck this cock for a very long time before I let you get off again. Is that understood?"

I clench around the plastic bottle and shift my hips, beginning to ride it, while I lick my lips and say, "Yes, Daddy."

Parking Lots

"**D**eeper," he says.

Jones holds the back of my head as he shoves his cock into my mouth, cutting off my ability to protest. Although I don't want to protest. This is unbearably hot.

His assault on my mouth continues, fucking me on one end as I ride the head of the bottle beneath me. My knees scrape against the floorboard, but I relish the tiny bits of pain licking up my body—my knees, my pussy, my mouth.

"You take my cock so well, Kitten," Jones purrs.

His voice is an erotic symphony I won't soon forget. I gargle on his cock as I attempt to say, *more Daddy*, and somehow, he translates. His hips gyrate while his hold around my neck remains unyielding. It's all I can do not throw up as his cock plunges down my throat, cutting off my air and dizzying my vision.

I sink onto the bottle as his pelvis hits my lips, both penetrating as deep into me as they can get. The bottle widens my pussy as his cock spreads my lips to the point that my cheeks might split. If they go any deeper, I swear they'll touch inside me.

Before I can fully comprehend how thoroughly fucked I am, Jones pulls out of me and shoves me down. My back hits the floor at the same time he tugs the bottle from my pussy, leaving me bare and thirsting. His palm comes down on my clit, slapping harshly as an equally unnerving smile lifts the corners of his lips.

"You've been a bad girl. I'm going to teach you a lesson and show you what happens when you misbehave."

Jones's gaze sweeps down my body hungrily and possessively. His eyes etch a trail into my skin that feels like a nail scraping down my body. My skin heats with every phantom touch.

"Please, Daddy," I say. I don't know what I'm begging for—an orgasm or simply to feel *more*.

His massive hand swoops down, grabbing me by the neck and tugging me up to my knees. I let my body go slack to hang limp, entirely at his mercy. Somehow, I know this is part of the role, and I willingly throw myself into it.

"I'm going to ruin you, Kitten," he smiles. "Open your mouth."

I do as he says, my jaw pops as I open wide. He pinches my cheeks. The look on his face should be a warning sign.

"Stick out your tongue," he says.

I push my tongue out, inviting him to fuck my mouth again. Whatever he wants from me, it's his.

He spits into my mouth and slaps my cheek. It's not hard, but it's enough to make my skin warm. When I go to close my lips, he pinches my cheeks again and spits into my mouth a second time. Pleased with whatever it is he's trying to accomplish, he lifts my jaw to close my mouth.

"Swallow," he says.

I gulp.

"That's a good girl. Keep being a good girl for me, Kitten," he says.

Then, as if he didn't just degrade me, he's cupping my breasts, pushing them up in a show of deceitful delight. Jones grips his cock, pumping it aggressively. Pre-cum beads at the tip, and he wipes it across my nipples.

"These tits are fucking gorgeous," he says.

My bodily juices leak onto the base of his car as he marks me, but he doesn't care that I'm making a mess. The door to his SUV remains open, allowing anyone who pulls into the parking lot a clear view of what's going on—how Jones is ruining me, how he's exercising punishment for my disobedience, and how much I'm enjoying it.

I stick my tongue out, inviting him to fuck my mouth again or spit in it. At this point, I don't care what he does as long as he uses my body. But Jones chuckles.

He's likely been in this very same situation dozens of times before. I ignore the insecurity creeping up my neck. The subs before me might have been hotter or better in bed, but I'll prove myself. I'll prove how well I can follow orders.

"Very good, Kitten," he coos as he lunges into the car, placing one foot on the floorboard so his cock is level with my face again.

He fists my hair and pulls my head back so far I'm forced to stare at the ceiling. The sharp sting of his hold radiates through me, making my pussy quiver. Jones's cock slaps me on the cheek, the mouth, the other cheek. He praises me, and before I know it, his cum is squirting across my face, leaking hot fluid into my open mouth, onto my eyes, and sullying my hair.

"You look even better with my cum painted across your face, Kitten." Jones's voice is as alluring as the devil himself. I lick my lips, tasting the sticky, salty substance that marks me. He pinches my cheeks, forcing me to stop. His grip hurts. "You like being a dirty whore, Kitten?" he asks, mouth parting slightly as he leans in and tucks away his cock.

I remain exposed and tainted on the floor below him. To any bystander, I would look like an abused little girl, a cum slut at the mercy of an evil man—which isn't far off. However, I'm far from it. I feel empowered and exhilarated.

"I like being whatever you want, Daddy," I say.

He smiles. "Such a good girl... I'm taking you for the weekend. You have ten minutes to tell whoever you need that you'll be unavailable but safe. I'm going to cover you in cum, not letting you rinse away my proof of pleasure until I've had my fill of you. Do you understand?" Jones emphasizes his point by rubbing his cum across my face and slapping my cheek, which makes a horrifically sexy wet smacking sound.

"Yes, Daddy," I agree.

His answering dark chuckle scrapes across my spine, making me even wetter. But his slow retreat makes my skin cold. Jones closes the car door, leaving me needy and desperate on the floorboards while he settles into the driver's seat.

We make our way back onto the highway in silence. Only once we reach cruising speed and I have buckled my seatbelt does Jones make a call on the Bluetooth speakers while I text my roommate not to wait around on me.

"Hello," a gruff voice answers.

"It's Jones. Entry for two, half an hour," Jones says.

"Will you be playing or observing?"

"Playing." Jones's eyes flick to me in the rearview, but his face gives away nothing.

What are we playing? Jones doesn't look back at me again as he continues making arrangements.

"Will you require a room?" the stranger on the phone asks.

"Yes—two nights," Jones states.

"Signed and tested?" they ask.

"No. Arrange it," Jones says.

"Done." The line disconnects.

Jones has me thoroughly confused and excited. "Where are we going?" I ask.

His gaze narrows on me as if that is reason enough, and he says, "You're about to have the best weekend of your life, Kitten. Now be a good girl, shut your mouth, lean back, and touch that pretty pussy of mine. I want you begging for my cock by the time we arrive."

I don't question him.

If there's anything I'm learning about this dom, it's that doing what he says is bound to lead to an unforgettable orgasm. I spread my legs, opening myself for Jones to watch in the rearview mirror as I slide my fingers through my sex, teasing and exploring myself, but never coming to orgasm as I imagine where he's taking me next.

His cum dries against my face and thighs. He's well on his way to painting my body in his seed.

Invisible Doors

We pull up to a nondescript building. Jones is clearly familiar with the place because he pulls into the alleyway beside it.

The only indication that this is a business is the logo of a red koala painted on the front door and a man sitting under an umbrella beside it. It's odd but no more strange than the short phone call I overheard half an hour ago.

Jones told me to be hungry for his cock when we arrived. After rubbing my clit for thirty minutes, and Jones making me stop every time I got close to coming, I'm more than hungry—I'm starving.

"Stay here." Jones gets out of the car, a confident swagger in his step as he approaches the seated man.

They exchange a few words before the man disappears into the building. He returns with a black silk robe, which Jones takes from him. Then Jones opens the car door for me.

"Here"—he motions for me to turn so he can slide the robe over my shoulders—"Follow me."

I do as he says, passing the doorman who takes Jones's car keys as we enter the black koala door. The hallway is as dark as the painted door. Only a dim light along the floorboards highlights the path into the building.

I can't be sure whether the air conditioning is cooling my skin or the danger of this situation is finally dawning on me, but my skin chills, goosebumps peppering my arms. My pussy is still aching from the lack of Jones's touch. This silk robe does nothing but heighten my desire to feel his calloused palms and thick cock again.

"This way." Jones places a hand on the small of my back, turning us right. The hallway ends, but he keeps walking toward the wall.

It's as if we're about to walk through it like something out of a fairytale when the wall shifts, opening automatically to expose a hidden doorway.

We step into a faintly lit room. The walls are black like every other wall and door in this place. The only color comes from a rich mahogany desk in the middle of the room.

A woman in her mid-fifties sits behind the desk, wearing a black robe similar to mine. She's flaunting gaudy gold jewelry on her neck, arms, and ears. Her silver pixie cut should clash with the gold. Instead, it appears perfectly curated.

"Jones. Good to see you again." Her words are impassionate despite their apparent familiarity. This is a strictly business type of woman. I immediately respect her.

"You as well," he says, leaning in and whispering something to her.

A sprig of jealousy wells inside me at the secret passing between them. But the woman nods in confirmation and opens a drawer, wordlessly sliding a black box across the desk. I tilt my head curiously, trying to get a better look, but Jones steps in front of me, retrieves the item, and slides the empty box back to her. A knowing smile graces her face as she finally regards me. It makes my stomach turn. But I'm not given much time to consider the situation because Jones is blocking my view of her. He's certainly playing into the mystery of this place.

"Relax, Kitten," he says as his hand slides under the robe's opening. I tense, and Jones arches a questioning brow. "Relax," he says again in a coaching tone.

His fingers slip through my folds, finally touching me, and I melt. He leans forward as if to kiss me, but when I close my eyes, ready to be consumed by him, he slips something inside my pussy instead. It's small and enters me easily, but it doesn't come back out. It sits firmly inside of me while also somehow pressing against my clit.

"Good girl. Now, just one bit of business before you can enter. Okay?" he asks.

"Okay," I say cautiously.

"Margot," Jones says.

Margot, the mysterious older woman, slides two stacks of paper across her desk toward me, and says, "This is an NDA and our standard policy agreement. If you have any questions, please feel free to ask now. However, I must insist you sign before allowing you to enter the club."

I look at Jones, who nods his head in confirmation.

"It's standard procedure. We have a very notorious clientele here. This provides security for everyone who enters, including yourself," Margot adds.

She points to a section on the contract and I step forward to read it. I skim the entire thing as Margot continues explaining.

"Many of our clients chose not to share their names or personal details of their lives inside the Koala Club. If you do so, it is at your own risk in particular situations. Please read those qualifying scenarios here," she says, pointing to another section of the contract.

Margot gives me a few moments to review the documents. Nothing about it looks much different than agreements and policies every business makes you sign when opening an account or applying for something, but it would take me an hour to fully read the contracts and absorb the information.

"The purpose of these contracts is to provide protection. This place allows people to become intimately familiar with each other but at a distance from their outside identities. Participation is completely consensual. As you can see, there are repercussions for clients who do not abide by the rules. The NDA and the agreement become obsolete for clients who break the rules or the law, which tends to deter anyone from breaking them," Margot says, motioning to the black ink pen.

My body grows cold in anticipation. I read over lines and lines of legal jargon. Most of it makes sense, but half of it is over my head. "So I have to sign both?" I ask.

Jones places a hand on my shoulder. "Everyone who enters signs, Kitten," he says.

"So you're signing one too?"

"I've already done so. Margot can fetch my copy if you'd like proof."

I shake my head. "No. No, it's okay. I'm not that worried." I say, reaching for the pen. I print and sign my name, then date each contract. It occurs to me I forgot to ask what type of club I'm about to enter. I didn't even read the description on the first page, but Margot gathers the paperwork before I can review it again.

"Very good. Now, please, wear this bracelet until you've seen the nurse," Margot says, wrapping a wristband around my arm.

"The nurse?" I ask. I feel like a deer in headlights. I can't seem to keep up with everything that is happening.

"You'll need a blood test for open play. Follow me," Jones says with a wink.

"Okay," I stutter uneasily, shifting my legs.

The object inside me moves, reminding me it's there, and I clench around it, hoping it doesn't fall out as I walk. I follow Jones, feeling it shift inside me with every step, rubbing against my inner walls and tickling my clit. It massages me in an entirely new way. Jones stops before the wall again—another invisible door, no doubt.

"Don't be nervous, Kitten. I'll take care of you. Trust me."

"Yes, Daddy," I say. The need in my voice is heady with desirable intoxication. I'm at this man's mercy.

"Very good." He smiles, then pulls out a tiny remote. He presses a button. The door opens as the object inside me buzzes to life.

"Ah!" I let out an excited breath that turns into a moan. The ache between my legs comes to life with a new fervor. Just when I think this can't get any sexier, I step inside the most sinful place I've ever been.

It's a sex club.

The Koala Club

Couches, beds, and benches are spread throughout the room, with naked bodies splayed across them. Soft moans of pleasure and the smell of sex taints the air. Men on men, woman on woman, men on woman on whoever, there are no limits here, as all types of people partake in the intimate act of fucking. The sounds alone have me sweating.

"Oh my god," I whisper, taking it all in.

Jones chuckles and turns up the remote, increasing the vibration inside me. I squeeze my legs together as I suck in a breath. Liquid slides down my thighs as the forbidden and foreign situation dawns on me. My body responds to it like a moth to a flame. Jones isn't a serial killer, far from it. But he might make my heart stop this weekend.

"Jones," I say.

His hand flies up to grab my throat, squeezing lightly but enough to cut off my words as he says, "It's Daddy or sir. Do you understand, Kitten?"

I nod despite my limited mobility. He lets go of my neck, sliding his hand down the front of the robe and opening it. The hemline skims back and forth over my hard nipples as the cool air rushes up to chill my body. I see the front of a pink vibrator pressing against my clit. *That explains it.*

"These tits are too pretty to hide. Now follow me, Kitten," he instructs.

I do.

Jones walks around the room, soaking in the erotic scenes playing out on each cushion. As I watch two men fucking a woman, I turn utterly liquid. The vibrator inside of me never stops coxing me closer to orgasm. As if it senses my desire building, it continually changes pace. It brings me close, then lulls me back down before I can come. It's infuriating.

"Do you like the idea of two men taking you, Kitten?" Jones asks, standing behind me and sliding his arms around my waist. He opens the robe further to expose my body to the room.

"Yes, Daddy," I respond, still watching the three people fuck.

The two men are holding the woman between them. Their cocks impale her on both ends. I don't know how she can take the one in her backside—his girth is visibly mouthwatering. He's even bigger than Daddy.

"Maybe I'll have someone join us," Jones says, running his hands up my sides to caress my nipples.

I'm transfixed, eyes glued to the people in front of me while my body presses closer to Jones behind me. His deft fingers slip the robe from my shoulders.

It drops to the ground, pooling at my feet. I'm as naked as the people around me.

While I'd usually feel embarrassed or uncomfortable being naked in front of strangers, I don't right now. Because I want to *feel* like they feel, their moans draw me in, making me want to do whatever they say to moan like that too. The men fucking the woman stare at me, watching as Jones's hands palm my breasts and pinch my nipples. They thrust harder, making the woman cry out.

"Let's play a little, Kitten," Jones says gruffly.

He spins me around and shoves me to my knees again. His shirt is unbuttoned, as is the fly of his pants. Jones is the only person in this room dressed, but he quickly catches up, unsheathing his erect penis. It's so fucking beautiful.

"Suck me," he orders.

I lick my lips and then impale my mouth with him, sucking him to the pace of the vibrations inside me. I imagine the toy inside me is another man. The thought of having two men inside me…I never thought I'd be the type of woman who could convince two men to sleep with me at once. But in this room, I feel like anything is possible.

"Luther. How are you?" Jones says.

I look up as I continue bobbing on Jones's cock. He shakes hands with a man over my head as if I'm not kneeling between them with Jones's cock down my throat.

"Doing well. I came to let off some steam. I see you have a new one—she's got a nice ass," the man comments.

He's a bit older than Jones but no less attractive because of it. Something about him screams extreme wealth. Maybe it's his towering height, or perhaps it's just his confidence. Either way, I'm drawn to it.

"Her pussy is even more beautiful. Want to have a look?" Jones asks.

My pussy clamps around the toy. Jones talks about my pussy like it's his to offer up and give permission to use. I'd be lying if I didn't admit that it was. This weekend, it's all his for the taking.

"I'd love to." Luther's baritone voice lowers an octave.

"Get up, Kitten," Jones says.

After one final suck of his cock, I stand. The men press in around me, not touching, but certainly not far enough to suggest anything innocent.

Jones bites his bottom lips promisingly as he raises the remote, switching the mode. The pulse intensifies, making me suck in a breath as my mouth opens. His fingers plunge into my mouth, forcing me to suck on them. I gag as his fingers touch the back of my throat and force my head back.

"Let's go to the bed in the back," Luther suggests.

"Good idea. Come, Kitten," Jones says, his fingers still in my mouth, hooking on my lower teeth and dragging me with him.

When we reach the bed, Jones removes his fingers and steps behind me, pushing me forward onto the bed. I fall onto it ungracefully.

"Ass in the air, sweetheart," Luther says.

I look at Jones for permission. He nods once, so I get into position. Turning my head, I watch as the men creep closer.

Jones removes the vibrator, and my wetness catches the low lights, my arousal glimmering on the toy. More liquid slides down my inner thighs as I clench around nothing, desperate to be filled.

"Fuck. Her pussy looks like it's never been fucked. Where did you find her?" Luther asks.

Jones chuckles. "You want to try her?" he asks.

"Fuck yeah."

Jones told me to enjoy it, so I don't question what happens next.

Luther flips me onto my back and kneels before me as Jones sheds the rest of his clothes. The man is utterly consumed with my vagina. His eyes haven't strayed from it.

Jones places a hand on Luther's head and pushes him forward. Luther eagerly obliges. His mouth encompasses me. I gasp as he shoves a tongue into my pussy. It's all I need to nearly combust.

"Oh my god," I moan as I catch sight of the wristband, and a thought races into me. "What about this?" I ask breathlessly.

"Luther," Jones says, addressing the man between my legs.

Luther looks up at the wristband. "It's fine. I'll wait for public play until you send me the results," he says as if that settles it.

I relax and raise my hips, pushing against Luther's mouth. I've never even spoken to this man, and yet, he's devouring my pussy already. It's so lewd.

His fingers find their way to my clit and my entry. He circles and inserts them. His movements are certain—just like his sexy confidence. Jones watches us, keeping a hand on the back of Luther's head, as he bites his bottom lip. He's enjoying this just as much as I am.

"Luther is good at eating pussy, isn't he, Kitten?"

"Yes, Daddy. He is," I answer, swiveling my hips against Luther's tongue.

Luther groans and rears back. He licks my cum off his lips. "She's divine. Are you sharing her?" he asks Jones.

Jones considers it for a moment. "Yes," he says nonchalantly. "My way, as always, though," he adds.

"Understood. I think she's ready now," Luther says.

He moves to the side, allowing Jones to center himself with me. His bare cock nudges my entry. I feel like I've waited a lifetime for this. He pushes into me. I eagerly tilt my hips to take all of him. As soon as his cock is fully seated, he pulls out.

My arousal sheens across his shaft and lower abdomen. I'm wetter than I've ever been. Jones shifts, and then Luther centers himself between my legs. I gasp at his size. *What is it with these massive male cocks around here?* Jones glares at me as if to dare me to deny him.

"Jones—" I begin, but he cuts me off.

"This is my pussy for the weekend, and I'll do what I please with it, including letting my friend here use it. Do you understand, Kitten?" he asks.

I gulp but nod. Tears pool in my eyes, but I will them away because my body aches. It aches with a need greater than I've ever had when Jones claims my pussy like this.

Luther's cock presses against me. It's nearly the same girth as Jones's but longer. When he pushes into me, they feel identical until he pushes another inch or two in. But eventually, there is no denying their difference as they stand before me, swapping places, shoving their cocks into me one thrust at a time.

It's so wrong, but it feels so right. They use my pussy like I'm just a fuck toy to them.

My arousal grows, making their dicks wetter with each entry. The men smile devilishly at me, enjoying the fuck out of teasing me with their cocks. It doesn't help that they are both so damn beautiful to behold. I feel like I'm in a dream. Never did I imagine two men this handsome, with cocks so perfect, would be taking turns fucking me.

"Her pussy is amazing," Luther comments, shoving into me and growling. Based on the furrow in his brow and the tension in his jaw, his release is close.

Jones takes my hips and shoves into me next. He's not gentle. "I know. I can't wait to take her ass. She'll be ready by the end of the weekend."

"You're staying the whole weekend?" Luther takes his turn, slamming into me with a grunt.

"Yeah. Are you?" Jones takes his turn.

My head spins. My pussy thirsts. They never stay inside me long enough for me to get off.

"Maybe I will, too, then." Luther rubs the tip of his cock over my pussy before sinking back in, taking it slow this time.

"I think she likes you. You're welcome to join us. Do you have a sub coming?" Jones smacks his cock across my clit, making me shiver, then pushes into me, circling his hips and stretching out my pussy.

"I can make it happen. Has she ever eaten pussy?" Luther asks.

Jones looks at me. "Kitten, answer Luther."

"No. I haven't, sir," I say as Luther takes his turn.

Luther grins. This time, he thrusts several times, finally giving me the sensation I desire. I reach up to grab his hips and beg him to stay, but he bats them away. "Oh, she is fresh, Jones," he says.

Jones puts a hand on Luther's shoulder. "I can't wait to ruin her," he says.

Luther steps off the bed as Jones pulls my hips to him, lifting me slightly as he plunges back into me and begins fucking me. I groan in relief but am cut off as Luther's cock chokes me.

"Not her mouth. Not yet. She likes it too much," Jones says.

Luther pulls out of me.

"Fine. Where can I come?" he asks.

"On her tits," Jones says, a smirk lifting the corner of his lip.

I should be humiliated by being used and cum on wherever these men want, but I'm not. Luther jacks himself off over my boobs, rubbing his precum on my nipples while Jones fucks me. Our sounds of pleasure fill the room, effectively making me a part of this house of pleasure community.

The men's hands find my body. Jones thumbs my clit as his thrusts turn frantic. Luther pinches my nipples as he jerks his cock. Before long and in synchronization, Luther's cock spurts cum across my breasts, my body tenses and shakes as I come around Jones's cock, and Jones fucks his cum deep into my pussy.

Our orgasm lasts what feels like a lifetime. And when Jones pulls out of me, I'm left feeling sated. The men lay down beside me, cum still covering my face, my breasts, and dripping down my thighs.

"This is going to be a fun weekend," Luther comments as he catches his breath.

"She's going to be filled with so much cum by the time I'm done with her," Jones says.

They chuckle in unison as Luther and Jones slide a finger through the cum on my chest, spreading it around like paint on a fresh canvas.

Service Charge

"Let me hear you purr, Kitten," Jones whispers against my ear.

The heat of his breath sends shivers down my spine. He and Luther brought me into a private room. It's the epitome of what I imagined a sex dungeon would look like and more. They have me trussed up on the bed. My hands are tied to ropes hanging from industrial-style ceiling hooks.

Luther and Jones pull the ropes, jerking me into a kneeling position. The silk sheet underneath me grows darker by the minute as the two men stalk around me, whispering indecent things in my ear. Their cum grows cold and hard against my skin.

"Monica will be here tomorrow," Luther says to Jones.

They keep talking to each other as if I'm not here.

"What's the hold-up?" Jones asks, skimming his fingers along an oddly angled piece of furniture resembling an uncomfortable horse saddle.

Luther strides up beside him, completely naked and seemingly comfortable with the fact that his cock brushes Jones's side as he stands next to him. I'm not sure if they're trying to tease me or if they're teasing each other. But the proximity of their bodies is doing so many things to mine.

"We have an agreement on days. Today is one of hers," Luther explains.

Jones grunts as if he understands this short lingo that confuses the hell out of me. I know very little about dom and sub culture. The extent of my knowledge goes as far as the minimal amount of research I squeezed in between my video chat with Jones and meeting him in person.

In my current position—literally and figuratively—I'd be considered the submissive. Granted, I'm happy to oblige. Jones's type of foreplay is hitting all my mental and physical erogenous zones.

"Sir?" I ask. The men's attention shifts to me, but their bodies' attention remains elsewhere.

"That's not the sound of a purr," Jones says. His tone is all venom and spice.

"Um…" I shift against the ropes, and they pull tighter, lifting me slightly.

"She didn't know you meant literally," Luther laughs.

"Apparently not." Jones stalks over to me. The pads of his feet leave deep impressions on the plush carpet as he makes a beeline directly for the bed.

He climbs gracefully onto it, kneeling before me yet still towering over me. Using a single finger, he draws a nail down the inside of my arm, carving a red line into my skin from wrist to armpit. My arm shakes involuntarily while goosebumps pepper my skin. I had no idea such a subtle taunt could elicit such deep need.

Jones leans in and licks up the side of my face. It's so carnal. He whispers a command, "Purr."

I purr, letting the deep, rumbling sound of satisfaction reverberate in my throat. His mouth moves to my neck, sucking, nipping, licking as if in appreciation for my obedience. So I purr louder. I didn't even know my throat could make the sound, but his tongue coaxes more of it out of me.

"She's a natural," Luther comments, coming to kneel on my other side.

Hands slide around my waist, digging into the soft flesh, as Jones's mouth moves to my breasts. He takes his time with each nipple, plucking it to an unbearably hard point. Any dried cum that was on my nipple is no more.

I want to wrap my fingers in Jones's hair as he sucks on me, but the ropes only pull tighter, lifting me higher from the bed. My knees lift off the mattress, leaving my shins to support my weight. My shoulders grow heavy and tight as gravity pulls me down and the ropes pull me up.

Luther's hand palms my pussy, pushing up with force to take some of the weight off my knees and wrists. He rocks my body back and forth, using his lower palm to grind into my clit.

Jones's mouth continues to venture down my body. His lips explore my hips, gently nipping down my sides. Each bite makes me jolt excitedly. But every time I move, the ropes tighten, inching me higher off the bed. The men adjust as I rise, doing their best to make me buck as if getting me to string myself up is a game to them.

"Let me hear that purr, Kitten," Jones says between bites.

I continue purring. However, it comes out like more of a moan as Jones's mouth moves to my lower stomach. His tongue flicks across my abdomen so low that it nearly brushes Luther's fingers.

I'm transfixed, my body eager and awaiting. Luther slowly moves his hand, keeping it flat against me as he nudges a finger into my entry, swirling it lazily. The weight of his touch triggers a deep aching inside me. It pulses in angst.

The need is catapulted into near desperation as Jones's tongue finds its way to the edge of my pussy. He flattens his tongue, running it alongside Luther's hand. I tense, yanking against the ropes so hard that they pull me to a stand.

But it doesn't stop the men.

Luther keeps his palm against my clit, guarding it from Jones's tongue. A single finger dips in and out of my pussy, teasing me. I purr—begging for more. Luther keeps Jones from licking me. He keeps him from touching that part of my body that wants him so badly. The men taunt and play with me like a toy.

Their movements turn into a synchronized dance of torture.

Just when I was beginning to like this type of foreplay, my body heats to what feels like ten thousand degrees. I'm sweating. My arms strain as the rope continues to inch me up, pulling me onto tip toes as Jones licks the edge of my pussy, peppering my inner thighs with sharp bites.

Luther presses his palm into my clit to appease the throbbing ache growing between my legs, but it only increases my desire. My purr turns into a howl as I buck my hips, trying to get loose from Luthers' chastising grip.

"Please," I whine.

The men chuckle in unison. They know this game far too well. They are professionals, and I'm a beginner. *What have I got myself into?*

Jones sits back on his heels as he regards me. The saliva from his tongue turns cold against my skin, making a fine companion for their hardened cum. But Luther's hand remains against me, his finger inside me.

"The more you want it, the harder you'll cum, Kitten," Jones says.

"You'll thank us for it later," Luther adds.

I suck in a shaky breath. There's no way I could want anything more than a release right now. I'm not sure what these men are doing to me, but the throbbing pain in between my legs is enough to know that I need it now.

"I need it now," I say.

"I know you do, but that pussy needs a little break. We're going to play with other things so it can get nice and juicy for us to enjoy later," Jones says.

I suck in a harsh breath as realization dawns. They aren't going to fuck me. They are going to make me wait while they…Play with each other?

Luther kisses my shoulder. The unexpected touch makes me tense. But then he slides his fingers through my sex. He takes as much of my slick heat as he can and rubs it up my backside, making me hot and wet as he probes my back entrance with a finger. Suddenly, I understand what Jones is insinuating.

"Wait. I can't do that," I say. Luther pauses with his thumb pressing against my tight hole.

Jones arches a challenging brow. "How are you going to take us both by the end of the weekend if we don't begin preparing you now, Kitten?"

His words bring heat to my cheeks. "Take you both?"

He doesn't answer my question. "Don't you want to be a good girl and please me?"

I gulp. They mean to take advantage of every part of me. It's so indecently hot.

"That's what I thought. Continue, Luther," Jones says.

Luther's hand slides back through my pussy, leaving me wanting each time he lubricates his fingers to drag the wetness up my backside. He never enters me, though. He only makes me want more of his touch, which makes me wetter. Jones peruses the room, acting as if Luther isn't making me wet beyond comparison, ruining the sheets underneath us.

"Relax, Kitten," Luther whispers, rubbing against my tight back hole.

I loosen a breath, trying to relax, if only because it's hard not to when the feeling he's creating only makes me thirst for more.

"Good," he says.

As he speaks, he slides one finger into me. The feeling is so foreign and yet so juicy. His finger slips in and out quickly. I push against his hand, aching for more of this unfamiliar touch. He's creating a beast of desire inside me.

"This one is needy, Jones. She'll be ready by day's end," Luther says, laughing as he slips another, girthier finger into me.

I groan. The pain and pleasure it brings are so unique that my entire body floods with a need so hopeless that there is no turning it off. The climax slams into me faster than I expect. Luther reads me and jumps into action. He pumps his fingers into my backside, and his other hand finds my clit.

He presses firmly into my front, rubbing harshly as his fingers plunge into me aggressively. I lose myself to him, slumping against him as my entire body shakes. The orgasm racks me. My cum coats my thighs.

With all these releases, a crude layer is building between my legs. Something happens, and the ropes release. I fall onto the bed. My chest heaves as I catch my breath, clutching my bound wrists to my chest.

But these men aren't going to let me off easy. Before I know it, Jones is plunging his cock down my throat. Luther stands beside him. This time they take turns shoving their cocks down my throat like they did in my pussy. I should be ashamed of the way they use me, but I only get more turned on in the hazy aftermath of my orgasm.

"I didn't say you could come, Kitten," Jones says, jamming his cock down my throat. I gag, but he holds the back of my head against him, making my eyes water before he releases me.

"She's a natural at taking dick," Luther comments.

"Hear that, Kitten? You're being a good girl taking our cocks. I might have to take a different approach with this one. She orgasms so easily," Jones says.

Luther winds my hair around his hand before he chokes me with his cock. I mumble, spit draining out the sides of my mouth, as I try to tell them I'll be good and listen. Jones is next, pushing his cock down my throat and holding me there.

I gag. And gag. And gag.

But he doesn't release me. Tears roll down my cheeks. I cry and tremble, tasting bile burning the back of my throat. My legs shake as if I can feel one of them fucking my pussy too.

Jones's cock swells, halting my gags. I focus, breathing through my nose so I can swallow him. His cum squirts out, but he's so far down my throat that I can't even taste it. My head goes dizzy with the desire holding me captive under this man. I'm at a complete loss of thought when he pulls away, leaving me to service Luther next.

They don't let me get off. Luther comes on my stomach, painting another part of me in cum while Jones fills every other part.

Dom Lessons

"Good girl," Luther says.

They lay me down on the bed. I'm spent—my body is exhausted, and my mind is incapable of thought.

"Do you want to take her upstairs?" Luther asks Jones.

"I will soon," Jones says.

The men settle into the bed beside me. Their breathing, once ragged, calms now that they've both found release. I can't say the same for myself. My heart beats wildly. However, the exhaustion and aftermath of my euphoric release keep me from voicing anything. All I can do is mentally replay everything that has happened today, but it only serves to make me horny and tired.

"Why do you allow your sub so many personal days?" Jones asks. His eyes connect with mine, holding the gaze intently as he and Luther speak as if to say *listen.*

"That's the arrangement. What else can I do? We can't all find such good subs like you, Jones," Luther says.

"You're supposed to be the one in charge, Luther."

Luther laughs. "Okay, master. Could you give me a lesson? How will you make this one yours on her off days?"

"First off, there are no off days," Jones says. "Second, it's simple—she won't go a day without thinking about me. Even if my cock isn't inside her, she'll be thirsting to please me."

"How?"

The men continue to talk. While I'm fascinated by their conversation, mainly because the subject matter is myself, I'm too dazed to interject.

Jones props his head up with his arm while the other lazily touches my body. His gentle touch soothes my racing heart. "On Sunday night, I'll take her home. She'll be so exhausted by the end of this weekend that she won't think anything of it until she wakes up Monday for work. I won't give her time to debate anything that happened this weekend. You can't let them deliberate their choices. Instead, I'll message her, telling her how much I miss that sweet cunt of hers and that Daddy has a favor to ask."

"I'm listening," Luther says.

"She'll be intrigued because I'm putting the power in her hands. So naturally, she'll agree. What's the favor? She'll ask." Jones chuckles.

Luther lets out a knowing laugh.

"I'll tell her I want a picture of her sweet little cunt every hour, on the hour, while she works. But I want her to wear a dress, and with every picture, the dress should slide further up her hips and stay there until the next picture. The first few hours, she won't think anything of it. She might get a little excited by sending me the photos, but it'll be quick, and she'll return to work immediately."

"I'm not seeing how this makes her yours every day of the week," Luther says.

Jones arches his brow in an invitation to argue, but Luther stops talking. "By the time she's finished work and has her dress lifted over her hips, sitting on her bare ass in her desk chair, and taking that last picture, I'll tell her she pleased me and that I have a reward for her. She'll spend all night anticipating and thinking about her reward. However, on Tuesday, I'm going to request that she does the same thing—send me pictures every hour on the hour."

"Are you testing your subs' patience, Jones?"

"Just listen. On Tuesday, she will be eager; her pictures will come sooner, and she won't be able to quickly snap the photo and move on to work because she'll be thinking about the reward and why I'm having her send me these photos again. And by the end of the day, I'll simply tell her she pleased me, and I have a reward for her."

"Your mind is twisted, man," Luther says.

Jones smiles. "On Wednesday, she's going to wake up angry with me because she hasn't been given her reward, and she's been too keen to please. Before her fury takes control of her senses, I'll tell her to go to her front door. There's a package waiting for her. She opens it. It's a massive dildo, twice my girth and longer."

Luther licks his lips. "Now you're getting somewhere."

"I know. So on Wednesday, I tell her instead of the dress inching up her thighs every hour, I want the dildo slipping into her cunt. No more or less than an inch every hour, or she'll be punished. She knows the terms, and since she's been waiting for me to get her off, she'll be more than happy to sit with a dildo up her cunt for eight hours."

"And this works?"

"If you'd quit questioning me, you'll find out exactly how it works," Jones scolds Luther.

"Fair. The floor is yours."

"Isn't it always? Anyway, this dildo is fucking massive. My little Kitten will have to work herself up a bit to get it in. As it always is in the first few hours, she can make do. But when she approaches the fourth hour, it takes a bit for her to relax enough to push through the pain of the dildo and shove it in four inches. But she'll do it. Because she still wants to know what that reward is. By the fifth hour, she spends ten minutes working the dildo in and out, making herself so wet that she's tempted to disobey me and fuck herself with it."

"You're a genius, Jones." Luther smiles deviously.

"I know. Once it's settled, she doesn't want to take it out. She might as well get used to the size since it's only going to go deeper. So she sends me the picture and leaves the dildo inside her cunt. As she works, every shift of her hips pushes the dildo deeper, and her body starts to adjust. She's seriously debating doing more than what I told her. By the sixth hour, she's soaked the dildo, and when she pushes it in another inch, her cunt sucks it in and gives her a taste. She sends me the photo with it six inches in, but I can tell by her pussy juice that she's been a bad girl."

I know I should interject. I should argue this truth. But to be honest, Jones has me as captivated as he has Luther. For some odd reason, I want his words to come to fruition. I want to know what it feels like to have this monster dildo inside me for eight hours, continuous torture to be fucked while I try to work.

"I tell her that her actions warrant punishment. She argues, thinking she can sway me by video chatting me. She's fucking the massive dong, thinking it'll seduce me. I tell her to stop, that her punishment is coming, and she better listen to me. So she stops. She doesn't get off. Even though all she wants is to come at this point, I tell her she can't come until I say so. Being the good submissive she is, she'll be disappointed in her behavior."

"So, on Thursday?" Luther asks.

"On Thursday, I don't reach out. But she still sends me the pictures of her pussy, sliding her dress up her hips, inch by inch, with the dildo going no further than I told her. She doesn't say anything at the end of the day. She tries to prove she's an obedient sub, even though I know she's not."

"And on Friday?"

"On Friday, she's mine. She receives her punishment. She'll be with me all weekend, just as I planned. And I'll get off harder than you ever have, knowing how badly she wanted me all week—knowing how I was on her mind every hour of every day. That's how you make a sub yours, Luther. That's how you give them no personal days. And eventually, they won't even want a personal day. They'll only want the days that have you in it."

"Brillant…" Luther says.

"Of course, that's not everything. You have to reward and take care of your sub eventually, like how I need to take care of mine. She won't last the weekend if I don't get her cleaned up. Help me take her upstairs."

"Sure. I'll get the doors."

Jones scoops me into his arms, and Luther drapes a blanket over me. I'm so lost in their conversation, in the promise of Jones's control and the ecstasy that results in it. Jones's warm skin and steady breath lull me into a microsleep as the men escort me into a plush hotel room.

Aftercare

I wake up to the sound of running water. "Jones?" I call for him.

There's no response.

My muscles ache and protest as I slowly roll off the side of the cozy bed. This room is different. It's modern and lacks personal artifacts, but it has all the comforts of an upscale hotel room. My feet drag me toward the running water. Steam billows around the door as I push it open. Jones is standing under the hot water, running his hands through his hair as suds of soap wash down his body.

He turns to me. "You should be in bed, Kitten."

"How long did I sleep?" I ask, drifting toward him. I'm not sure if it's Jones or the water I desperately desire.

"At least sit down. You're shaking like a leaf," Jones says, pulling me onto the handicap seat in the shower. He redirects the shower head to pour over me.

The hot water pounds into my achy muscles, the heat seeping deep into my core. I never knew sex could make a person sore like this. I suppose I've never had so many orgasms in one day, though, nor have I ever pleasured two men at once. So, my knowledge of how exhausting sex can be is clearly limited.

"How are you feeling?" Jones asks as he squirts soap onto his fingers.

"Sore," I say.

"The first weekend is always the roughest. You're not in shape for this sort of thing, but we'll work on that."

I peer at him curiously. *The first weekend?* But I don't ask the question.

"Tonight, I'll rub the soreness out so it doesn't linger. But don't expect my touch to always be this gentle. Do you understand?" Jones says.

I nod, too tired to debate.

"Good," he says, lifting my arm and massaging the soap into my skin.

A groan slips out of me as soon as he reaches my shoulder. The tension eases with each swipe of his thumb over my muscle. The ropes holding me up did a number on my back muscles. But before they fully relax to his touch, Jones moves to the other arm. Then my legs. Then he's pulling me to my feet to rinse my hair.

After a solid thirty minutes of soapy massages and hair washing, Jones signals we are done with a pat on my ass before he retrieves two towels.

This feels so domesticated. It's so at odds with his dominant personality, and I'm not sure if I love it or hate it. One thing I do know is that I need it if I'm going to have sex like that again soon.

"Come here, Kitten," Jones says, holding the towel out for me while his rests comfortably around his waist.

"Thank you," I say, as his arms wrap the massive plush towel around my shoulders. He steers me toward the bedroom.

"I'm sending someone in to take care of your hair. We'll want it pinned up for the weekend. They'll also cater to your nails and skin, then finish with a massage. I have some things to attend to, but I'll return when they finish. Oh, and a nurse will come in at some point." He mindlessly rattles off the plans he made for me while dressing.

I want to ask what catering to my nails and skin means and where he's going. But I know this isn't my role. I contacted Jones to enlighten me—sexually, not emotionally. I'm here to receive pleasure, to let go, to have enough orgasms to make up for my abstinence the last six months and my impending abstinence for the foreseeable future should he find me undesirable after this weekend.

On the off chance this thing with Jones lasts a while… I'm not really sure what our agreement is. He insinuated more weekends of pleasure, which I am fully onboard with. But sometimes physical intimacy leads to emotional intimacy, and that is entirely off the table for us. I'm happy to take it in strides and see where it goes, but even men get attached. It's not always the woman who wants to pursue *more*.

After Jones leaves, the assistant styles my hair in two french braids. She cleans my nails and files the sides so they aren't too sharp or long while a nurse takes my blood. Lastly, she buffs my skin. It's so polished that it shines. I've never had skin this shiny.

When she finishes, she leads me into the living room portion of my accommodations. Apparently, Jones booked me a suite.

There is a massage table in the center of the room. The curtains are drawn, setting a dark, sensual mood, while soothing nature sounds complement the musky scent of incense.

Soundlessly, a therapist directs me to the table while my stylists leaves. I never dressed—not having the option with my lack of luggage—so I lay down naked under the thin sheet.

Cool air prickles the top of my exposed shoulders as the therapist presses on different parts of my body. He takes his time pressing, moving, rubbing, and stretching me.

I'm not sure when it happens, but eventually, I fall asleep under the masseuse's touch. All contemplation is effectively put on hold while my body rests and prepares for the remainder of this weekend.

Table for Two

Jones returns with a pep in his step and a fresh suit on. He strolls into the room like a tidal wave. I'm immediately caught in his gravitational pull, my gaze sweeping over his perfect facade—dressed to the nines like he's going to the symphony. His eyes narrow, regarding me momentarily before they crease on the edges, and a smile warms his face.

"Put this on," Jones says, tossing a garment bag on the bed beside me.

"Okay." I shuffle toward the side of the bed despite my body's protests to continue relaxing after my much-needed pampering.

If every weekend with Jones includes endless orgasms and a visit to the spa, I'm ready to sign a contract that says I'll be his fuck toy for life. That is, if I can stand long enough to get through it. My side cramps as I try to sit up.

Jones pauses and gives me another sideways look. "Are you okay?"

"Yes," I lie.

There is no way I'm letting him know just how sore I am. Not yet, at least. My body could become one with the bed right now. It feels so mushy, but I'm determined to power through it because the ache reminds me of what's to come.

"Let me help you." His tone is soft as he takes my hand and helps me rise from the bed. "We need to work on your fitness, Kitten. You won't be able to handle back-to-back weekends like this if you don't start exercising."

"I never knew working out was so important for sex," I joke.

He smirks sexily. "There are many things you don't know about sex."

"I can't exactly argue with that."

"You'd be ridiculous to try," he says.

His hands slip under my silky black robe. He slides the material from my shoulders, letting it fall to the floor as he unzips the garment bag.

I'm not sure why he even brought the outfit in a garment bag. It looks ridiculous hanging there, mostly sheer material that could ball up in the palm of my hand. It's skimpier than any lingerie I've ever worn, and since I'm already naked, we might as well get right to the fucking. Why bother with straps and itchy fabric?

"What's that for?" I ask.

"Dinner," he says.

Dinner? Obviously, this isn't my usual weekend hang-out, but I'm confident the lingerie Jones is holding is not dinner-appropriate attire.

Seeing the confusion on my face makes Jones' face light up. He laughs. His mood is surprisingly lilt—an odd transition from his moody, bossy attitude in the bedroom.

I like both sides of him—a lot. At least, that's what my body keeps telling me as my thighs press together. I want to rip the tie from his neck and beg him to choke me with it.

"Dinner is at the K-club. Minimal clothing is encouraged, and aphrodisiacs are the only things on the menu," Jones says, slipping the slip over my shoulders.

The nude fabric slides down my skin, snagging on my breasts and hips. It leaves nothing to the imagination. The sheer fabric shows every tiny detail of my nipples as it presses into them. I'm grateful the tightness of the fabric provides some lift to my breasts, but otherwise, I feel bare. The nude color disappears into my skin, making it appear like I'm not wearing anything.

"Perfect," Jones says, admiring my body by running his knuckles up my side and over my breast. He tugs the end of one of my braids playfully.

I stifle a moan and bite my lip as I ask, "What are you wearing?" He points at his current attire. "You said minimal clothing is encouraged," I say, realizing this is a common trend—me naked and Jones dressed.

"Yes, it is encouraged. You're the eye candy tonight, Kitten, not me."

A blush creeps up my cheeks as I imagine what Jones has in store for me tonight. I'm naive to think we'd be staying in this room to fuck all weekend. He's definitely taking me back to that club. Not that I'm complaining; there are still a lot more things I'm curious about.

"Let's go," he says.

I follow him out the door and into a dimly lit hallway. My nipples harden from the brisk air. My heart is already racing, paranoia creeping in one beat at a time as diffidence takes over my thoughts.

The hallway looks like a typical hotel until we cross paths with another couple. The woman is decked out in all leather, holding a leash attached to a collar around the neck of a man following her. I've never seen anything like this before. Jones has shown me new ways to experience pleasure, but I debate if a collar would excite me. At this rate, who knows? So far, he's proven that I know little about my desires.

We push through a large metal door and descend on the stairs. Barefoot and barely covered, I easily troll after Jones. The wood floor chills my toes, making me creep closer to Jones for warmth. We aren't the only ones making our way down, but I hear faint conversation and sensual sounds all around us.

Three floors below our suite, we enter the K-club.

It's the same as I remember upon first arriving. However, some details escaped me as I was lost in a haze of lusty desire as soon as Jones and Luther came onto me. The mere reminder of what we did has my core heating. This place…Will it ever not make my heart stop? It's something out of a dream. Or, more likely, a nightmare. There's nothing ethereal or gentle about this place. It could very well be the gateway to Hell. And if it actually was, I'm certain it'd be just as packed as it is now.

"Just over here, Kitten." Jones directs us to an empty booth.

Booths are strategically positioned around a raised stage, confirming my suspicion that dinner at the K-club is *more* than just dinner. A waitress comes around, and Jones orders drinks and appetizers for us both. I'm happy to let him order and purposefully ignore their conversation so I can watch the people filtering into the other booths.

This is the most diverse place I've ever been—racially and sexually. Nothing is off-limits here.

Jones might be the most modestly dressed person in this place. He's perfectly at home in his suit while other people flaunt their bare skin like it's the latest thing walking down runways.

The fashion is as diverse as the people. Chains, ropes, and metal barbs are as prevalent as my light, innocent garb. Boobs and cocks of every shape and size imbed themselves in my memory. Frankly, I'm mesmerized and beginning to feel like I'm having an out-of-body experience. This world is so unlike anything I've known before. This is the type of thing I imagine only happens in books and movies. Yet, I'm living it in real life. And everyone looks so happy, so satisfied, and comfortable. It's as if they've been waiting all week to come here and are finally free to express themselves.

"Calm down, Kitten. The show hasn't even started," Jones says, running his hand up my inner thigh.

His fingers press against my center, pushing the fabric between my legs to stick to the wetness between them. "Sorry," I whisper, not sure what I'm sorry for other than knowing I'm going to soil the bottom of this slip if he keeps touching me like that.

"Nothing to be ashamed about, but you'll have a hard time sitting here if simply watching people take their tables turns you on this much. I don't want you too sore for tomorrow."

"I'm not sore," I lie. My vagina is achingly sore. Except being in this place makes that soreness turn hot. I can disregard the pain for more pleasure.

"Liar," Jones says, sliding the fabric up so my pussy is fully exposed.

With the table in front of us, only we can see my sex. He slips his fingers through my folds, coating them in my juices—proof of how turned on I already am. My head falls back against the booth, and I moan. *Fuck it.* I won't be the first nor the last to moan in this booth.

"That won't do," he says, withdrawing his fingers to admire the wetness.

It's so sensually sexy. "Sorry," I say again.

The waitress returns, setting down our drinks as Jones licks his fingers clean. She doesn't even bat an eyelash, as if this is the least erotic thing she's seen all day.

"Cheers." Jones clicks his tumbler of amber liquor against mine and takes a sip, not waiting for me to pick up mine. He's so dominant and carefree it makes my bones chill. Before I do something uncharacteristic and ask to suck his dick or ride his cock with everyone watching, a low, rumbling beat blares over the sound system. "Pay attention," Jones says, pushing my drink toward me and wrapping an arm around my lower back.

I lean into him as I sip the chilled liquor. The lights dim even more than they already are as people take the stage. And then the show begins.

The scene being performed isn't just erotic but artistic. The way their bodies move is an expression of pain and plea-sure—much like how I currently feel.

As the two performers undress each other, their gentle touches are perfectly measured to draw the audience in and trap us. When their clothing is entirely removed, a chair is brought out. The man leads the woman to it and motions for her to sit. She sits. He spreads her legs, exposing her glistening folds to the audience. The spotlight zeros in between them, highlighting her womanly form. Her confidence captivates me.

Taking his time, the man kneels between her legs and kisses up her thighs. Then, the stage begins to rotate so everyone in the room can get a complete visual of her pussy.

The man takes his sweet time, letting us absorb the shine of her arousal building between her legs. My body silently begs for him to touch her already. To taste her. To please her. My feet tingle with the urge to go up there myself and take a shot at getting her off, even though I've never been with a woman before.

The female performer's body quivers on the chair as the man teases her. His cock is hard and lays against his leg, but still, he takes his time, not touching her where she most needs. He licks across the arch in her foot and she bucks in the chair. He sucks in her toes, one at a time, and she cries out as if that alone is going to make her come.

Jones' hand maneuvers its way between my legs, making me jolt.

"Lean forward, Kitten," he says.

I lean forward, pressing my breasts against the edge of the table. The stiff side digs into my nipples. I rub them back and forth, letting the rough edge scrape against my peaked nipple.

Jones pats my ass, indicating I should lift my hips. I do.

As the man on stage finally opens his mouth and sticks his tongue into the woman's pussy, Jones's fingers slide through my sex.

He drags my wetness backward, circling my asshole. I'm too lost in what's happening on stage to care what he does to me though. He's going to take my ass eventually, and right now, I'll let him do anything to me.

The man on stage ravishes himself on the woman. Her hands are in his hair, pulling him against her as her hips grind into his face. His hands dig into her thighs, pushing them apart so he can drive his tongue deeper into her.

Meanwhile, Jones continues to take my desire and slide it backward between my buttcheeks. I'm sitting on the edge of my seat, relishing in the performance and Jones's long fingers stroking me.

When the man on stage stands and fists his cock, Jones adjusts himself. My stomach tightens. I lift my hips higher, aching for Jones to insert himself in me as the man on stage is about to insert himself into the woman. As the man penetrates the woman, Jones's finger penetrates my backside.

A moan releases itself from my lips as I lean onto the table, giving him a better angle to fuck my asshole. His finger pushes into me each time the man on stage thrusts into the woman, making me even hornier. My pussy aches and clenches to be filled, but Jones has other ideas.

"Brace yourself," Jones says, withdrawing his fingers.

I turn my attention away from the stage to see what he's doing. His fingers palm a smooth object. I shift, but Jones straightens my hips.

"Stay still, Kitten. Be a good girl, and I'll reward you."

I hold still as he pushes the object against my asshole. It's so much thicker than his fingers but also so much more delightful. I turn my attention back to the stage.

The performers have switched positions. The man is sitting as the woman rides him. She takes her time, rising to the top of his cock before dropping back onto it. Her ass bounces each time she drops onto him, and her head falls back. She audibly displays how good his cock feels inside her. I want that. I need that.

Then, as if reading my thoughts, Jones slides the plug into my ass and twirls it. I feel so full, yet so empty. He tugs on the plug, making my muscles clamp around it. He uses the object to fuck my ass, working it in and out, twirling it around. It fills me yet massages me. It hits a part of me that's never been touched. It makes my pussy wetter, and soon, I'm dripping onto the leather bench below me.

The woman on stage stands and turns around. She faces the audience as she continues to fuck the man. His hand is on her clit, rubbing it. The twisted look on her face tells me she is close.

Jones shifts, guiding my hips onto his lap. His erection digs into my wet center. The plug sits nicely in my backside, moving inside me every time my hips shift or press into Jones's erect cock. I lean back against Jones's chest. His fingers find my clit, mimicking the performance on stage.

This feels better than I ever imagined. I'm lost to the sensation of my ass being full and my pussy empty. But the woman's pussy being fucked raw is enough of a visual to stimulate me. My cunt pulses and squeezes as my backside tightens around the plug. Jones fiddles with my clit expertly.

"Come with her, Kitten," he demands.

When the words leave his lips, the woman on stage cries out. She loses control, but her partner doesn't. He fucks upward, slamming into her so harshly that the only sound in the room is the pounding of their bodies. Liquid squirts out of her, spraying the stage, the man's hand, and his cock, but he doesn't stop fucking her.

I lose it. I cry out as my pussy bubbles with cum, seeping out as the orgasm drains me.

"Yes, Daddy," I moan.

"Yes, Kitten. Tell me," he coos into my ear as his hand plays with my wetness.

"Thank you, Daddy," I say quietly. I feel Jones smile against my cheek.

No Limits

“This is going to be easier than I thought," Jones says.

I lean back against the leather cushion as my panting slows. Even though my orgasm has faded and left me sated, the female on the stage hasn't lost any rigger after her release. She shifts her hips on top of the man with more energy and ferocity than before. I begin to understand why Jones is so concerned about my fitness level. One Jones-level orgasm, and I need a break. But she continues to fuck, her body savoring the effort.

Her skin sheens with sweat, yet she continues to move, showing no signs of slowing down. It's as if she's only just found her rhythm. The man seems perfectly content to let her do all the work until one arm slides around her stomach, and he flips her.

In an utterly perfect maneuver, the man kneels behind the woman, holding her legs up while she balances on her arms. He penetrates her in a reverse doggy-style move that quickly becomes the next thing I want to try.

I don't even notice the appetizers being brought to the table. The performers on stage fully enrapture me. Everything about their bodies is utter perfection—the way they have sex is no exception. My new goal is to fuck like that.

"Enjoying the show?" Jones asks while dressing an oyster. He extends it to me instead of taking it for himself.

I take the oyster and slurp it down. The delicate balance of sweet, spicy, and salty fills my mouth—it's another kind of sensual heaven.

"Thank you. And yes, I'm loving this…Is that okay?" I say, unsure of myself.

The last thing I should be asking is if my enjoyment is okay. I recently had two men in my bed. It was far more scandalous than anything I've done before. Plus, I'm just a bystander right now. Why shouldn't I shamelessly enjoy it?

"Anything goes here, Kitten. Don't be ashamed of what turns you on. Bask in it. Own it… I'd be concerned if you weren't enjoying the show," Jones chuckles, but his face turns serious. "There are a few things we should discuss. I've started this relationship off a little different than most. Frankly, I didn't think you'd adapt so quickly and easily to the submissive role nor enjoy it so clearly."

"Okay," I say, picking at some invisible dirt under my fingernail.

Jones tilts my head up. "We need to discuss boundaries."

I'm not entirely sheltered to the point that I don't understand boundaries. Unfortunately, after what I've experienced today with Jones, I'm not sure there is a boundary I don't want to explore.

He continues, "This is the part where you tell me your limits, Kitten,"

"I don't know that I have any," I say.

Jones chuckles again. The sound rattles my brain, making me completely senseless.

"I can't argue with that, mainly because I love a woman without boundaries. I've already noticed how curious you are.

We can figure out your limits together. Anytime you feel uncomfortable, you can use a safe word. Commonly, people like to use red, yellow, and green to communicate their limits. Whenever you feel uncomfortable with something, say *red*, and I will stop immediately. Say *yellow*, and I will venture slowly. Say *green* or say nothing at all, and you give me the go-ahead. Make sense?"

"That makes sense," I say, accepting another oyster from Jones. He seems perfectly content feeding me while he goes hungry. "Aren't you going to eat?"

"I'll eat when you're done. You need more energy than me, Kitten."

It's hard to argue with that. Plus, it feels good having Jones take care of me. While his punishment was brutal and extreme earlier, it was also satisfying and exhausting. I've read about edging, but it's way more intense than I imagined. The articles don't do it justice. I don't plan to be on the receiving end of any more punishments, but if I am, I'll need the strength. If part of being a submissive is getting this royal treatment—baths, massages, and hand-fed oysters right before having mind-blowing orgasms—I think I could get used to this.

The performers on stage shift again as a third person joins them—another man. The men hoist the woman between them and impale her on both ends. I quickly imagine myself, Jones, and Luther in the same position. They already promised to take me together—is this what it will be like?

I watch, enthralled. The woman's eyes roll in the back of her head as the men take their time with her. One goes in. The other pulls out. One pushes in, and the other pulls out. Her body moves like a wave, taking one cock in the front, then the back.

My body clenches around the object in my behind every time the man behind her pushes into her asshole. My pussy clenches too, but nothing fills it. The aching need promises to make me sore despite anything entering me tonight.

"Jones… I mean, Daddy," I say absentmindedly.

"Yes, Kitten?" He looks at me as he dresses another oyster.

His bossy, perfectly curated facade is so hot. "I won't be sore tomorrow. I can handle it, please."

Jones arches a brow, lifting the edge of his eye and highlighting the masculine cheekbone below it. He *tsks* at me as he pinches my chin between his thumb and forefinger. "Oh, Kitten. The show just started. Are you that hungry for my cock already?"

"Yes," I say, licking my lips and tasting salt.

Jones releases my chin, motioning toward the corner. The lights are too dim to see what or who he's calling over, but they quickly reveal themselves as they saunter over—a man and a woman. They look like twins.

I expect Jones to make an introduction when they arrive at our table, but no words are exchanged. Instead, they crawl under the table. Jones unbuttons his pants and pulls out his half-erect cock.

Delicate fingers wrap around the base of his cock. I lean back to see more of what's happening beneath the table and find the twins sucking him off.

"Oh my god," I say, smacking a hand over my lips to hide my shock and smile.

I can't look away. I don't know what type of foreplay this is, but when Jones plants a hand on my stomach, pushing me back into the cushions, forcing me to sit back and watch, the aching in my core transcends anything I've known before.

"Wait. Is this a punishment?" I ask, suddenly realizing he's not letting me have him.

This has to be some form of torture, and I don't understand why I'm receiving it.

I want to be down there. I want to be sucking his cock with them.

"A, lick my Kitten's sweet cunt for a minute. I want her juices on my cock," Jones says.

My mouth gapes at the demand in his voice. The male twin jumps into action. He spreads my legs and dives into my lower lips before I can utter a word or tell him to stop. I should be on my knees pleasing Jones, but right now, Jones is making two people please us—together.

The ache spreads across my body, and the instant his tongue delves into my folds, I'm jelly. I let out a low moan as I grind my pussy into this stranger's face, winding my hands into his hair and holding him against me.

"A, back to me," Jones commands.

The twin releases me with one final lick, then plunges his mouth down onto Jones's cock, choking on him. His face glistens from my arousal as he paints Jones's cock with it. I may be Jones's submissive, but Jones is playing dom to two other subs, and I get to be privy to the pleasure without doing any of the work.

I groan, aching to touch my pussy while I watch this strange man and woman suck him off, but I get the sense that Jones disapproves of me giving myself orgasms. My orgasms are his to deliver—no one else's.

We continue like this until the performers finish and a new pair comes onto the stage. Jones bosses the twins—A and B—around, making A suck my clit and tongue my pussy before going back to deep-throat Jones. I nearly come undone four times, but Jones senses it and makes A pull away before I can get off. He's edging me again but making someone else do the work. It's making my head spin.

By the fifth time, Jones says, "I think it's time we finish this so we can get back to dinner. Are you ready for the main course, Kitten?"

"Yes," I say breathlessly.

"Finish me," he says.

He's giving me his orgasm, showing me I'm his primary. His orgasms are mine, just as mine are his.

The twins crawl out from under the table, retreating as silently as they arrive. Jones rests his arms across the back of the booth, letting me know he's waiting. I'm eager to please and desperate to finish, so I lean down and suck him into my mouth.

It's easier than the time before. I'm learning his size and how to take him deeper.

I suck him hard, not caring who watches or how spontaneously dirty I've become. I suck him off like my very life depends on it. It doesn't take long before he's holding my head down, coming down my throat. I slurp up every ounce I can get as my body screams at me to mount him next, but I know I can't—I have to wait.

When I sit up, Jones readjusts his pants, putting his dick away. I lick my lips, cherishing the taste of him.

"Good girl," he says. "Let's have a bit more to eat, then you'll get your release."

His orgasmic promise is everything. The aching in my core settles and moistens, awaiting his promises of pleasure as I consume every bite of food he offers me.

Pleasure Planning

With the promise of an orgasm in the back of my mind, I'm in a rush to return to the room, but Jones seems content with taking his time. We stop in corridors along the way back, watching various scenes play out. Every pleasure imaginable, every position, every combination of genders, takes place under this roof.

This place—The Koala Club—is a pleasure house where nothing is off limits.

I'm learning a lot from watching others. Jones seems unaffected by the sensual heat transpiring around us. But I'm a wet mess. Everything excites me.

The longer my release is withheld, even the most perverse things begin to excite me.

A woman trussed up against the wall, with clamps spreading her pussy apart, nearly undoes me. The man controlling her body takes his time, touching her innermost parts with tools and objects that don't look like they are made for the bedroom while she's spread wide for everyone to inspect. The sweat on the woman's body tells me they've been at this for hours.

I can't imagine how hard the orgasm will hit her when he finally gives it to her. I never thought that waiting could improve the pleasure, but it does.

The teasing, the edging, the neglect. It does something to your entire body and mind. It makes the ache spread to places you didn't even know could ache for pleasure. And when the one delivering that pleasure touches you, touches any part of your body, the sensation quadruples in intensity.

I find myself touching my body as we watch other people. Jones is careful not to let me touch my pussy or get off, but he lets my hands wander elsewhere. He lets me skim my fingers over my inner thighs, along my waist, and the other sensitive parts of my body.

As we watch another couple hiding in the dark like Jones, Luther, and I last night, Jones stands behind me, replacing my fingers with his. I breathe a sigh of relief at his touch. His softly calloused hands and agile fingers seem to know the exact amount of pressure to deliver and the most sensitive spots to touch.

"What do you think of this place, Kitten?"

I regard his question seriously. While my own perverse excitement repulses part of me, the other part feels free. Why should I be ashamed of exploring my sexual desires freely? I've been walking around basically naked for hours, and no one has looked at me or made me feel less for doing so. Most people would likely shun a place like this, but I've never felt more liberated.

"I like it," I say honestly.

"Good. If this weekend goes well, I'd like to keep you for a while. What do you think about that?"

"What do you mean by keep?" I still have much to learn about this relationship dynamic, but *keeping* sounds more akin to slavery.

"It means you'll be my only sub. We may take on other part-ners here, but you'll be my only true sub. I won't engage in sexual intercourse without you present. Outside of my relationship, of course," Jones adds.

His relationship. A fun fact I conveniently keep forgetting about. "So you'll sleep with your wife, too? But I can't sleep with anyone else unless I'm with you?"

"Not likely. We enjoy different…things. But I won't be dis-honest about the possibility should things with my wife change," Jones says.

"Okay," I say, mulling over his offer.

It's not like I can refuse it, and it's not like I have any other prospects currently. I already knew he was married, and I'm al-ready sold on the orgasms. I don't care who he fucks or when he does it, but if him knowing who and when I fuck is part of the role, I'm perfectly fine agreeing. For now.

I've needed a dom daddy like Jones in my life for far too long. We have no ties to each other. No promises. The deal we made was only about pleasure and will continue to be only about pleasure and respect. Selfishly, it's exactly what I need right now.

"Okay. I accept," I say. "So, do I get to have a say in who you fuck here?"

Jones laughs. "If it upsets you, just say the word. But we'll always fuck people together, Kitten, and you'll like seeing my cock in other people. I can already tell you're a hedonist."

I've never thought of myself as anything or capable of falling under some sexual kink term, but he's right. Watching the twins suck him off was so sexy. Plus, they were servicing us both, and Jones's end goal was for me to get him off.

Everything we've done thus far has ultimately been about me. I'm sure that will change at some point, which might mean watching him get balls-deep in another woman, but nothing about that bothers me.

It'd probably be hot to watch his cock disappearing in another woman's pussy before he uses her cum to fuck me. My spiraling, curious mind is turning this genuine conversation into foreplay.

"I trust you," I say.

"Good. Trust is essential in this relationship. Now, let's go back. I think I've made you wait long enough," Jones whispers, sliding his hand under the sheer dress.

His hand cups my pussy, his fingers on the edge of my entrance. I'm already slick for him, and a moan escapes me as I lean back against his chest.

"So needy, Kitten. Let me hear you purr again."

I purr—a soft trilling that only we can hear. Jones nips my ear delightfully.

"Beautiful," he says, slipping a finger inside me while his other hand bobs the plug in my backside.

I'd nearly forgotten it was there. My mouth drops open as he finally lets my pussy clench around something. His finger sinks into me as he chuckles devilishly.

"Let's go," he says, dropping his hands.

I slump and groan, but a warning glare from Jones tells me to shut the fuck up if I want my orgasm. I'm forced to hide my smile at the playfulness. I know I've been good tonight.

He leads the way back to the room. He doesn't touch me again, nor speak to me. We silently enter the room. He points to the bed, and I follow his direction while he pours two glasses of water. I sit on the edge of the bed, waiting for him.

Jones takes his time, setting the glasses on the bedside table while discarding his suit jacket on a nearby chair. He unbuttons his shirt and places it on top of the jacket. There's a stain on his pants where my pussy was grinding into him earlier. He notices me staring and smiles.

"My horny little pussy. I love seeing everywhere your cunt has been, Kitten," he says.

I bite my lip, trying my hardest not to launch myself at him while he continues to undress.

Finally, he says, "Stand up, Kitten."

I stand.

Jones approaches me. Our bodies are close but don't touch. The heat ruminating off of him sears my skin. I want to jump on him, rip his pants off, and beg him to fuck me unconscious, but I don't.

His hands glide over my waist, cupping my buttcheeks as he stares down at me. There's so much intensity in his gaze. I feel weak at the knees but swallow the dryness coating my throat and steel my nerves. His eyes are frosty as his finger slips inside me, and the other takes hold of the plug.

In unison, his fingers go to work. As one finger enters me, he tugs at the plug, making my body move in a dance to find the most pleasure.

I fall into Jones' chest, searching for more heat, more pleasure. His arms press against my stomach and my back as he works me from both ends.

It's not enough, though. I need more than one finger and more than a subtle tug. My body has become accustomed to being owned by this man, and his gentle prodding drives me to insanity, not pleasure.

"More," I plead, looking up at his determined face.

His lip quirks up on one side. "At this rate, Luther and I will be stuffing our cocks in your ass by the end of tomorrow. You're so needy for more. Aren't you, Kitten?"

If it feels this good, I can only hope so.

Jones gives me more. He inserts another finger while pressing his palm against my clit. This time, his movements are more aggressive, giving me the friction I desire. Instead of jostling the plug like before, he pulls it out and begins to fuck my asshole with it, showing me what it really feels like.

Within seconds, my body is shaking. I spread my legs wide, begging for more. Jones concedes. He kneels before me, working the plug and his hand within me. I plant my hands on his shoulders, barely able to keep upright as his fist pounds into my pelvis and he drives his fingers into me.

He leans down, engulfing my clit with his mouth. He's fucking my pussy and my asshole so hard, I know I'll bruise, but my body wants more.

"Yes, Daddy. More, please," I cry out.

His teeth scrape my clit, sucking me into his mouth so his tongue can flick across me. My body tightens, then turns to liquid as I combust. But Jones doesn't stop.

He licks me. His fingers fuck me. And the best, most tantalizing part of this—he fucks my ass like I've never been fucked before. He treats my body like a vessel for pleasure.

Cum spurts out of me, running down his hand and his mouth, but Jones still doesn't stop. He works me, bringing wave after wave of ecstasy to my body. When bright spots blur my vision, Jones lays me on the bed.

He slowly pulls the plug and his fingers out of me, using his tongue to clean up my cum and slowly work me down from the sensation, making my body entirely too sensitive. I shake involuntarily—as if I'm detoxing from drugs.

He climbs over my body, kissing his way up my stomach and breasts. His gentle appreciation elicits shivers down my arms and my neck.

"Good girl, Kitten. How was that?" Jones asks, planting a kiss on my forehead. He lays beside me, pulling me under his arm.

"Amazing," I say, laying my head on his chest. I'm barely able to speak, and sleep takes me quickly.

Restraints

J ones is gone when I wake up. I'm not sure whether he stayed the night. By the lack of personal items around, including his clothing, I decide he didn't.

It doesn't bother me, though. I've never been one to stay the night, either. It creates an unnecessary, fake level of intimacy between two people who have no intention of creating a relationship beyond sex.

He followed through on his promise last night, and I slept like the dead. And it's not like he didn't think of me even after delivering on his promise. I woke to find my phone plugged in beside the bed, fully charged, as well as ice water and expensive-looking lotion.

I take a long drink of the water, not realizing how thirsty last night's activities made me. Then, I take full advantage of the heavenly-smelling lotion, smoothing it over my skin and taking extra time to rub it along the parts of my body that are worn from too much aggressive friction. Thumbprint-sized bruises pepper my arms and hips, so I take extra care in those areas.

Jones's thoughtfulness would surprise me coming from most men, but this isn't his first time. He knows the toll *his* kind of sex takes on a woman's body.

His care doesn't stop at the water and lotion either. The bathroom is outfitted with all the necessities, and the armoire is stocked with several scandalous clothing options. It seems he's been busy this morning. Does the man sleep?

Breakfast arrives as I shower and rub more lotion into every aching inch of my body. It's a feast for at least four people. Either Jones is planning a calorie-exhausting day for me, or I'm having guests.

I don't wait to find out as I help myself to a large portion. I'm starving. It feels odd to stuff my face with fruits and sausage while scantily clad, but no one is present to judge. It's not every day a woman finds herself in this very position—treated to countless orgasms and pampering from a man she recently met online. Never in my wildest dreams did I think a random online meeting would spiral into this.

"I like your choice."

His voice makes me jump. I turn around to find Jones leaning against the door jam to the hallway. He walks in, and the door slams shut behind him, making my skin twitch. The man's nearness is enough to put me in the mood.

The things he did to me last night…It wasn't anything out of the ordinary—other than the sex club and making two people kneel beneath a table to service us—but the way he did it had my body screaming for more.

"Thanks," I say, setting down my fork.

Jones takes the seat across from me and fills a plate. "Don't let me stop you. I see you're taking my instructions well. You'll need your strength today."

I certainly hope I'll be needing the extra calories today. If more calories equal more orgasms, I'll pack snacks. "So… What's the plan today?" I ask, biting into my omelet. This breakfast is Michelin star-level quality. I can't imagine what Jones is paying for it.

"Luther and his sub, Monica, are joining us for breakfast soon. Then, we'll go to the club. I reserved a room for us."

"A room?"

"Yes—a playroom."

Jones is as curt as usual. It would irk me, but I know this is part of the role and developing the necessary level of trust we must put in each other. Plus, the mystery will add to the pleasure. I'm beginning to like his teachings and all the surprises that come with them.

"Okay," I say as someone knocks on the door.

"Let them in," Jones says.

I immediately get up to open the door. Dressed in jeans and a vintage t-shirt, Luther stands behind a pretty dark-skinned woman. His hand is planted predatorily on her shoulder.

"Hey there, beautiful, ready to play?" Luther asks.

"Yes," I say shyly, unsure how to answer the man who talks to me like Jones but isn't.

This whole dom relationship still confuses me, and my disconcertment only seems to please Luther. He strikes me as the kind of man who likes mind games. In contrast, Jones is the type of man who wants total subservience and communication. I'm glad I got the latter.

Luther slaps Monica on the ass, and she gets moving, rushing into the room and taking a place at the table. She slips me a wink when we all take our place at the breakfast table.

It's weird doing something so normal while knowing we're about to get majorly kinky with each other. We all know the inevitable is coming—we're going to fuck each other. Yet, we casually eat our breakfast as if we're old friends. It'd be laughable if the result weren't so damn satisfying.

The men talk while leaving Monica and me to our own devices. But we don't speak. We just smile politely at each other.

She's a beautiful woman. I wonder what it would be like to have skin as luminescent as hers or a face that looks like it belongs on billboards. She must get laid as often as she wants, which makes me wonder why she's here.

I guess we all have our reasons. I'm only just discovering this world, and I doubt I'll soon forget it. Without Jones's connection, I'm not sure how I'd have become a part of this community. On the other hand, Monica was probably flagged down on the street and personally invited in.

After breakfast, Jones and Luther decide it's time to leave. They lead us down the dark hallways, but we don't go to the club on the ground floor this time. Instead, we climb the stairs. Jones uses a key card to open a black door with a red handle. Everything in this place is red and black. It adds to the dark sensuality.

They let Monica and I enter the room first. It's designed like a dungeon. My heart jumps erratically, beating frantically as I skim over the various equipment dispersed throughout.

Jones speaks softly so that only I can hear him. "Remember the stoplight we talked about?" he asks.

"Yes," I say, recalling his instructions last night. Red means *stop*. Yellow means *take it easy*. Green or don't say anything to *continue*.

"You say the word, and we stop. It's important to remember we have control of the situation. Without complete consent from all parties, nothing will be done. Do you understand?"

His words comfort me as I stare at a big wooden X that looks like a torture device. "Yes," I say.

"Good. Now go stand at the wall." Jones points to a wall with bolts in it. Cuffs and carabiners hang from the bolts.

I do as he says, and he follows me. It doesn't take a genius to figure out what he plans to do, so I lift my arms and spread my legs before he tells me to. His proud smile tells me I assumed correctly and will be rewarded for my agreeableness. It turns out my minimal research is paying off.

Jones buckles the restraints into place, securing them at my wrists and ankles. They match perfectly with the lingerie I chose today.

I'm wearing a black strappy bra and thong. Except, it isn't your typical underwear. The clothing purposefully has holes over my nipples and vagina, allowing easy access.

He tests the straps, pulling them tighter so my backside is forced against the wall. I test the strength, trying to pull away, but they hold. The last strap goes around my waist. He tightens it to the point that it's digging into my abdomen, making it hard to suck in a deep breath.

"That's tight," I say, coughing as my body adjusts to breathing shallowly.

"Good," he says with a smile as he slides an appreciative hand over my breasts, teasing my nipples until they harden. "You're going to watch as I fuck Monica, Kitten."

"What?" I wiggle against the bonds; sad I'm being left out already when I was such a good girl last night.

"I like it when you're needy and jealous, aching to prove yourself," Jones cups my jaw, lifting my head.

I ignore him, staring at Luther and Monica. Luther is tying her up, too, but in the middle of the room, leaving her exposed on all sides. Unlike me, whose back is pinned against the wall.

"I'm ready to prove myself now," I say, returning my focus to Jones.

"Is this a hard limit for you, Kitten?" Jones asks seriously.

"No," I say quickly.

It's not a hard limit, as far as I know. Although, jealousy and desire are already raging inside me. However, waiting to suck him off last night was worth the wait. I loved watching the twins ready him for me to slurp down his cum.

"Good. Don't take your eyes off of us."

Jones returns to Luther and Monica. He and Luther stand before her, stripping their clothes and tossing them aside. When their cocks are out, Monica's eyes latch onto them.

Mine do, too.

Voyeur Vexation

Jones and Luther are mesmerizing to behold. Ridiculously tall. Confident, verging on arrogant. Smooth skin of drastically different tones. I'm not sure if the universe has been listening to my prayers, but it sure seems like it when I look at the two of them.

"The honor is yours, my friend," Luther says to Jones. The two men speak as if they're the only ones in the room.

"You flatter me," Jones says as he circles Monica menacingly.

He picks up a braided whip and skims it across Monica's inner thigh. She whimpers even though he's barely touched her.

I track Jones as he teases Monica's body, feeling phantom touches on my skin that follow the line of his touch on her. He skims the outside thigh as he circles her, moving to her backside. Then he lashes out, slashing the whip across her lower buttcheek in one quick movement.

She cries out and bucks against the chains holding her but doesn't tell Jones to stop. She seems to relax into the chains after every lash. A red welt rises to the surface of her skin, and I swear my buttcheek heats in response.

Jones continues slashing the whip across Monica's body. He focuses on the tender skin of her inner thighs and low buttocks, leaving red marks in his wake. But they fade eventually. His whips are harsh yet forgiving.

The sting heats Monica's skin, bringing a flush to her cheeks, but it fades when Jones glides the flogger between her folds. Sweat slides down the side of her face as a breath rushes out. She sinks into his touch.

I begin to understand this dance as moisture pools between my legs. There's a thirst that must grow, making us damn near desperate for release before it can be quenched. The thirstier you are, the more satiated you'll be. True gratification comes from hitting rock bottom.

Jones and Luther bring us to the bottom. Kicking, screaming, crying, it doesn't matter. They'll drag us there if they have to because that's their job. And although our bodies may protest and our minds may flounder, ultimately, we trust them. We trust that the end result will be a form of compensation far greater than the protest to get there.

Luther grabs a pair of black clamps from the bench where Jones retrieved the whip. "She's ready, Jones," he says.

Jones takes his leave, tossing aside the whip and stepping back for Luther to take his turn. Luther is gentle with his touch. He kisses the fading red marks on Monica's skin, making her shiver. As he kisses her breasts, he blows on her nipples, making them peak. Then, he puts the clamps around them.

I clench internally as I watch them. I've never had nipple clamps placed on me, but my body can imagine the feeling. As Luther kneels between Moinca's legs, doing something to her clit, Jones sneaks up on me.

"I wouldn't leave you out completely, Kitten," he whispers as he places the same clamps on my hardened nipples.

I stifle a cry as the pain shoots through my center. My abdomen flexes, trying to bend forward, but the restraints keep me still.

"Oh my god," I say, as the pleasure rolls down my spine, soaking my pussy.

The sharp sting of the clamps is never-ending. Jones chuckles and pulls on the cord between them. This time, I cry out, the pain and pleasure racking my body.

"Please," I say, unsure what exactly I'm begging for—to get them off or to give me more.

"In due time, Kitten. In due time."

He returns to Luther and Monica, leaving me gasping through the tight pinch on my breasts. It takes all my concentration to breathe through the pain.

Luther sucks on Monica's pussy. She cries out and bucks her hips, but the chains hold her in place. His fingers are plunging into her front and backside. I recount Jones doing the same to me last night: the feeling, the pleasure. The mere memory is nearly too much to handle.

Just as Monica and I are about to find simultaneous release, Luther retreats, leaving Monica panting. There's a clamp on either side of her pussy, pulling it apart with straps around her legs. I've never seen anything like it.

My orgasm halts before it can crest. I'm waiting for her. I need the visual to get off without the touch.

Luther blows on her wet cunt, and she whimpers. Her heavy-lidded eyes plead for more, and Luther is happy to oblige. He stands and shoves his cock between her pussy lips, aggressively rubbing against her until he bends his knees and angles upwards. Luther grabs her hips and uses the leverage to drill into Monica.

He's not gentle, but her loud groans tell me she's close. He tugs on her nipple clamp, then twists the side. I assume he's tightening it as a tear slides down Monica's cheek.

Luther slows his thrusts when Jones steps up behind her.

"Get your cock wet, my friend," he says as he pulls out of Monica.

Jones slips into her next. I fully expect jealousy to take over every emotion inside me, but it doesn't. Desire, hot and heavy, radiates within me as I watch Jones intentionally take Monica.

Her head falls back as the intoxicating feeling of Jones's cock reverberates within me. His eyes are focused on her with an intent that ignites a fire within my belly. Jones fucks as if it's his sole purpose in life to deliver orgasms. After last night, I believe it.

When he pulls out of her and steps back, his cock glistens. Monica is soaked, even I can see it from the far end of the room. I want to be jealous. However, I'm far more eager to be next.

Luther aligns himself with her once again as Jones positions himself at her backside. I can't believe what I'm about to witness.

Even though I watched it last night, my dom wasn't partaking. My dom wasn't showing me what he plans to do to me eventually. The reality of this situation settles into my bones. The promise of pleasure is an intoxicating drug that has me in a chokehold.

Jones and Luther pull on Monica's leg restraints, loosening them so they can lift her. Their arms raise her legs, spreading them so they can take her at the optimal angle while allowing me the perfect view to see their cocks entering her. I'm sweating with anticipation.

Their cocks nudge at her holes. Slowly, they sink into her. Monica's satisfied groans fill the room. Jones turns his head to watch me as he rolls his hips, taking Monica's backside.

Both men's cocks pump in and out of her, rocking her body back and forth as they take her. Jones's gaze is locked on me as he fucks this other woman. I've never been privy to anything so hot.

"Harder," Luther says.

Jones complies. His fingers dig into Monica's thighs as he rails her from behind, and Luther rails her from the front. Monica takes it like a little fuck doll.

I want to feel what she feels. I squirm in my restraints, but the shifting only causes tingling in my nipples from the clamps. The pain is so intense I swear they're going to rip my nipple off.

An occasional splatter is the only sound accompanying Monica's moans and the men's fucking. She comes loudly as the men's pace becomes unbearably rough.

Luther's cock is covered in it when he pulls out. Ropes of white sticky cum slide down the shaft of his cock.

Jones withdraws and takes a seat on the bed behind them. He's no longer watching me but becoming a spectator as well. I wish he'd do something to me. Anything. Pain. Pleasure. It doesn't matter at this point. I'll take any touch.

Luther circles Monica, taking Jones's position behind her. "I'm not done with you yet, baby," he says as he shoves into her ass.

Monica cries out but takes it.

She never tells him to stop or slow down. Instead, she makes it look pleasurable. And maybe it is pleasurable.

Maybe anal is one of the many things I've been missing out on in my sex life…Leading me to online dating and the mysterious Jones. It's like one of those life milestones that you'll never really understand the feeling of until it happens. It's an awakening of sorts. A sexual awakening.

Her orgasm surges to life. She cries out as Luther grunts behind her like a rutting animal. He pulls on the nipple clamps with one hand and slaps her pussy with the other.

My body aches in ways I never thought possible as I watch them. Jones sits behind them, cleaning his cock with a wet cloth. His cock stands up, clearly turned on by this. I want to ride him, but he won't even look at me now.

They leave me on the edge of the playroom, only allowing me to watch. My body becomes so twisted with need that I'm bound to burst at the first touch.

Luther stills inside Monica as her cries slowly fade. He stays inside her as he unbuckles the restraints around her wrists. She crumbles toward the floor, but he catches her, still inside her ass. He walks her to Jones, keeping her mounted. I'm impressed by his strength.

Holding her legs apart, Luther fluidly sets her down on Jones's cock. Monica falls against Jones's chest as the men fuck her again.

An entirely new feeling stirs within my core. It's like she's boneless as she flops around, her body exhausted and energy waning. The men have her, though. They support her body, allowing her focus and energy to remain on the pleasure.

I'm entranced, my body aching to be used. And when Monica kisses Jones, I lose it.

My orgasm flares to life as I watch them kiss, watch them fuck. Jones breaks the kiss and watches me tremble in my chains, fluid leaking out of me to pool on the floor. He's never kissed me on the lips. I don't even know the feeling, but damn do I want to.

He laughs knowingly. "Do you see this, Luther?"

Luther continues fucking Monica while he looks at me. "Coming just from watching? She's insatiable, Jones."

"I know. Suck my cock, pretty thing." Jones pulls out of Monica, scooting up the bed so Monica can suck his cock while Luther fucks her.

They take their time with her, rubbing, fucking, and touching while Monica sucks Jones. When Luther pulls out to clean his cock, Jones tugs Monica around, positioning her pussy over his face so they can sixty-nine.

When his mouth engulfs her, her sucking becomes frantic. She chokes on his cock as Jones licks her. Meanwhile, my body feels like a fucking wildfire. What he does to her is what I need him to do to me.

Luther walks over to me, watching them as he strokes his dick. "Are you jealous, pretty girl?"

"Yes," I say. It's not jealousy, but we can call it that. It's need. It's desire.

"Jones, how long will you leave her like this?"

Jones's words are muffled as he replies while eating Monica out, "Bring her over."

Luther unfastens the restraints and leads me to the bed. I sit next to Jones and Monica, who are still sixty-nining. I should be jealous, but I only envy not being part of it. Jones spreads her thighs and says, "Come here."

I crawl to the head of the bed, kneeling beside Jones's head as he buries his face between Monica's thighs and then comes up for air. "Lick her," he says.

I lean in and lick Monica's pussy. I've never tasted a woman before, but I'll do anything Jones says. She's surprisingly tasty—her juices are sweet. Jones smiles below me as I continue to lick her.

"Sit on my face, Kitten. Let me taste you with Monica still on my tongue."

Jones doesn't need to tell me twice. I've waited long enough to be touched. Monica moves to the side, still sucking Jones's cock as I sit on his face. He wraps his hands around my thighs, pressing me down as his tongue plunges inside me. Luther stands on the bed and shoves his cock down my throat before I have a second to consider what's happening.

Suddenly, we're all performing oral. It's so naughty. Monica sucks Jones. Jones licks me while I suck Luther. If only Luther were licking Monica, we would all be connected somehow.

My hips grind against Jones's face as my head bobs on Luther. It takes all of a minute for me to orgasm. Jones shoves Monica off his cock, coming across his chest as Luther pulls out and spills himself onto my face.

I grind my pussy into Jones's mouth appreciatively, knowing he saved his cum for me. I'm his sub, and only I get his cum.

Tribe Vibes

A final drop of cum beads at the tip of Luther's cock, and I lick it off before he steps off the bed. "I need a break," he says with no appreciation as he walks away.

Jones pushes my hips up gently and says, "The girls can play for a bit."

I slide off of him, feeling the lingering touch of his fingers on my hips while Monica goes to clean the cum off his chest. Jones stops her with a hand.

"Wait. Monica, clean up Luther's mess," Jones says.

Monica nods. She grasps my face and begins licking me. Her tongue glides over my lips, my nose, and my cheek, slurping up every drop of Luther. His cum is hers. Just as Jones's cum is mine.

When she's finished, Jones says, "Kitten, lick up my cum, and don't leave a drop."

I do as he says while Monica sits on her heels, watching me and waiting for her orders. I take pride in knowing Jones saved his cum for me.

"Have you ever been with a woman, Kitten?" Jones asks as I finish cleaning up his cum.

He nods at Monica, and she moves beside me. Gentle hands guide me back against the pillows. Her hands slide up the front of my thighs, spreading them apart.

"I haven't," I answer.

"Monica, teach my girl how to eat pussy. She'll need the lesson for later tonight."

My heartbeat races as the promise of doing something new tonight drifts through my imagination. I'll need to know how to eat pussy? How hard can it be? I know what feels good for me, so figuring it out can't be too difficult.

Monica pushes my legs further apart as she lays between them. Her movements lack the command Jones bestows. I like how gentle her approach is. It's so at odds with the two domineering males. Luther kneels at the end of the bed, watching us, while Jones lazily strokes himself beside us.

"I recommend taking your time with a woman," Monica says, "It's all about coaxing the orgasm slowly, letting it build before she comes."

Her soft fingers trail the inside of my thighs. My heart is pounding now. Other than my gynecologist, I've never had a woman down there. Monica peppers kisses along the crease between my thigh and vagina.

The nearness of her lips makes my breath catch completely. She looks up at me, a devilish smirk playing on her face.

"You want to explore every part of her with your tongue. Make her understand that you're enjoying it as much as she should be."

Monica's breath chills my sex as she speaks, making me pucker. "Okay," I say as my legs shiver.

My nerves don't deter her, though. Her fingers spread my pussy. She assesses me to the point that I swear she's studying me, memorizing every fold and curve to remember later.

"You have a beautiful pussy," she says before diving in, her mouth engulfing my clit.

I gasp when her tongue slides up the length of me. She makes a show of it, keeping my lips spread and using only her tongue as she runs it through my lower folds like a cat cleaning itself.

Every time she reaches my clit, she sucks me fully into her mouth, flicking her tongue across me. My legs instinctively tighten. My thighs grip her face, keeping her tight against my cunt. Monica shoves my thighs down and holds them apart so she can continue her taunt.

"Be a good girl and let Monica be in control, Kitten. Otherwise, I'll have to punish you," Jones warns.

I look at him. His cock is fully erect. His knuckles turn white with the death grip he has on it. I reach out to help him, but he smacks my hand away.

"Learn how to eat pussy properly, and then you can have my cock," he says.

Monica's fingers loosen on my thighs and slide upward. Two fingers dip into my sex, curling, and pumping, while two more find my clit, circling. I'm pulled away from Jones as her expert fingers make my body shudder.

Her tongue and mouth go to work on the area between her hands. Every part of her does something different. And somehow, I feel every bit of it. From the rolling of her tongue to the pressure of her fingers. One slight movement at a time she brings me closer to euphoria. It's so gentle, yet so damn satisfying.

"Yes," I say, winding my hands in her hair. It's incredibly soft, just like her skin.

Instead of the coarse skin of a beard or the rough pads of a man's hands, she's all soft and silky. Her skin glides across mine easily, massaging and kneading without causing tenderness. It's so provocative. So entrancing. I never want anything but the supple curves of her lips on me.

Monica's fingers increase their pressure. Her fist bumps against my entrance as she begins to pound, not pump, her fingers into me. She lifts her head so I can watch her fingers work as her tongue laps up my arousal.

"Come on my face," she says between licks.

I try to respond, but words escape me. She rubs harder.

That familiar tingling sensation warning me of an orgasm spurs to life. Monica feels the tightening inside my body and switches gears. She nips my clit, causing a spike of pain to shoot up my spine, making my head light as my body tenses.

I fist the sheets underneath me but can't deny the headrush that rolls down my body. Then, Jones tugs on the clamps, and I explode.

My back arches off the bed as a cloudy, sticky substance coats Monica's fingers. She doesn't stop. She coaxes every last drop out of me, refusing to stop until my body sinks into the mattress. Every tense part of my body loosens and releases.

As the post-orgasm bliss takes over, Monica climbs up my body, lazily moving her fingers in a circular motion while she kisses up my abdomen, appreciating my curves. For some reason, the way she worships my body is so much more glorifying than when a man does it.

She's a woman. We're our own worst critics. We don't miss the thigh dimples and bumpy skin. I've admired her body and appearance all day—not noticing a single blemish that didn't appear absolutely perfect—but never thought she might think the same about me. It's the biggest compliment I've ever received.

Suddenly, her mouth is on mine. We kiss each other. It's soft and sensual, so unlike kissing a man. Her lips press gently against mine, sliding across my skin like water as we explore each other.

Monica straddles my leg. She pushes against me; the feel of her lower body mushing with mine is like butter until she begins to grind, and I understand what the hype of being with a woman is all about. Monica lifts my shoulders, pulling me up and shifting our bodies as she leans back.

"Find the spot that feels the best," she says.

With her legs on either side of mine, her hips swivel, searching for the sweet spot. I do the same. Our bodies rock back and forth, and side to side, as we stimulate each other. Our frenetic movements moisten my lower body.

The scent of our arousal is a spicy aroma. I lose myself to the passion. My head falls back, eyes closed, as my focus narrows on that *feeling*. The friction spurring at the apex of my thighs hums with delight as I find it.

My core tightens insatiably. The fact that we can bring each other to orgasm without a dick is a fun new experience that I can't wait to explore more.

"Watch her, Kitten," Jones says.

His command forces my eyes open. I watch Monica. I watch as our bodies grind together, and damn, it's hot. The sensuous rolling we do to rub our pussies together sends me over the edge.

Monica's head falls back as she moans. Her body goes still, then trembles as her hands fist the sheets now.

I mirror her, losing myself to the shockwaves of an orgasm that was once a fantasy but is now my reality. I could do this all fucking night.

Eiffel Tower

Jones lowers me onto the bed and removes the clamps. I'm fully sated, but my body still buzzes intensely. His hand kneads up my sides, tugging at my skin in an infatuating rhythm that hurts momentarily before a soothing warmth spreads across the area as his mouth follows his hands. I close my eyes as Jones massages me. I lose track of his mouth and his hands.

All the pressure in my core evaporates as I melt into the bed under Jones's touch. He's gentle and purposeful. The slightest increase in pressure, the intentional flick of his tongue, is all an act with a single intention. Regardless, any doubt I had is absolved by his aftercare.

I sink into the sheets, giving way to unconsciousness. But it isn't long before Jones lifts me. He pulls me into his arms, walking me across the room. My eyelids flutter in the blissful afterglow of the last twenty-four hours as Jones hoists me onto a chair. No. A leather saddle.

He slides me to the back and gently lowers my stomach onto the awkward furniture. I'm straddling it, teetering slightly on the narrow beam.

"What is this?" I say.

"It's a saw horse, Kitten. It will help Luther and I open you up for tonight."

"Tonight?"

"Yes, Kitten," Jones says as he adjusts my body and begins cuffing my wrists and ankles to the base of the legs. "I told you that you would be taking both of us by the end of the weekend."

"Oh," I say, feeling a blush creep up my cheeks.

Jones chuckles. It must be amusing to watch my inexperience continually shock me.

"Relax as much as possible, Kitten. And tilt your hips into the pad, not away from it."

I do as he says. Jones scrapes a fingernail down the spine of my back, forcing my hips to push even more into the pad. It takes the pressure off other body parts.

"Good girl. That's where I want you."

He walks around me, circling me, checking the restraints binding my body to the saw horse. When he's content, he stuns me with a quick slap to the back of my thigh. It stings. The sharp pain radiates up my leg, settling between my legs. I squirm, but the bindings keep me in place.

"This should be fun," Luther says.

The men are standing behind me. With my wrists bound on the legs of the saw horse, I'm unable to turn. I'm not sure where Monica went, and only Jones and Luther's voices indicate where they stand.

"Get the pinwheel," Jones says. The baritone in his voice looms over me, giving way to sensory memories that make my heart jump. After some shuffling, I assume Luther returns because Jones says, "Relax and trust me, Kitten."

"Okay," I say quietly, more to reassure myself than to answer.

"Remember your words—red, yellow, green. Do you remember?"

"I remember."

Jones takes whatever the pinwheel is and glides it over my lower thigh. It still stings from his slap earlier, but when the little pinpricks puncture my skin, I buck in the saddle.

Thankfully, the saw horse keeps me anchored so the device that feels like needles doesn't pierce too deeply. My focus narrows on the object slicing across my skin. My heart races, forcing me to pant. I'm two seconds from yelling *red*.

"Am I bleeding?" I ask. My heart beats so wildly that I think it might explode.

"Kitten… Unless you ask, I'll never bleed you. You're not ready for that. What color are you at?" Jones asks.

"Yellow," I say.

Luther turns my head to face him as he kneels beside me. He cups my cheek while my other digs into the leather cushion. My breath is hitched. I can't get enough oxygen in as my mind twists, fear latching onto that little prickling pain running up my thighs toward my pussy.

"Deep breaths, love. Do it with me," Luther says. He inhales for three seconds and exhales for the next three.

I focus on breathing, following Luther's lead, and when my chest finally decompresses, Jones begins. This time, the pinwheel—as he called it—is hot against my skin. It's deliciously warm, and when it pricks my skin, entirely new sensations well inside of me.

Now that I know the needles aren't puncturing my skin, it feels more like they spring off me. They bite into my thighs just enough for the resistance of my skin to kick back and for Jones to pull away. My legs smolder from the heat of the pinwheel and the tingling each spike leaves behind. My breathing relaxes, but my head feels light. Adrenaline rushes toward the sight of pain.

Luther strokes my cheek as Jones moves further up my thighs. My breath catches when the blazing device touches the highest, innermost part of my thigh.

I choke on my inhale, unable to focus on Luther's deep breathing exercise as Jones barely touches the tender skin above my clit with those sharp points. My vision blurs as a crazed energy rolls over my body. I become pliant, succumbing to anything Jones decides to do next.

"That's it, Kitten," Jones coos.

Tears well in my eyes. I've never cried during sex. I don't even know why tears are forming, but they do. When I blink, one runs down my cheek.

"You're so pretty when you cry, sweetheart," Luther says, wiping the tear away with his thumb.

He wraps my braids around his fist, pulling tight to lift my head off the bench. More tears slip down my cheeks. It feels like he's going to scalp me while Jones slices off my skin. Then, an ice-cold prickling touches the same spot between my legs.

I suck in another breath from the surging fire Jones has lit within me. He continues his assault as I lay anchored and helpless, tears streaming down my face as the sting in my scalp turns into a fiery pain while the chill piercing my clit makes my entire body tense.

The hot, the cold, the tiny little pinpricks beckon the blaze forward. The heat between my legs is growing insatiable, quivering needily. I want to devour something. Anything.

As if in answer, Luther tugs my head back even more, making my neck strain. He fists his cock with his other hand and thrusts himself into my mouth. Jones drops the device and rubs the smooth, round head of his penis against me. I want to sigh in relief, but I'm gagging on Luther's cock.

When Luther drops my hair and pulls out of me, I slump against the sawhorse, disheveled and breathless, trying to put myself together, but Jones buries himself inside me before I have a chance to recover.

His cock spreads me and fills me. After making me wait all day to receive him, my reality fragments within seconds. Jones has a way of amplifying this feeling—his hands, his mouth, even his cock knows exactly what to do. He swivels his hips, burrowing inside me, as his fingers dig into my ass.

"Luther, the plugs," he says.

Luther retreats.

I can only imagine how the two men standing behind me look. Jones slips out of me but doesn't leave me long. He runs two fingers through my crazed lower half, sitting viciously wet and still thirsty.

Two fingers slip inside me, then continue gliding up my backside. He presses his fingers against my asshole, forcing me to open. It feels as if I am tearing, but Jones works his way in slowly. I don't dwell long on the fullness of his fingers as the erotic act sends me into a euphoric haze.

Jones works a warm object against my backside, removing his fingers and replacing it with something thicker. I give way to the object as he finesses it into me. As he does, he pushes his bare cock back into my pussy.

Luther rounds the table, stalking toward me. Without so much as a word, he replaces my panting with the slick sound of his cock choking me.

With vivacious certainty, the men take me zealously. Tears stream down my face as Luther refuses to yield. He captures my breath as he pushes deeper into my throat.

Jones's feverish disregard for my squirming sets me on edge. He shamelessly shatters all my thoughts as he rewards me. It's well worth the wait.

I can barely breathe. I can't see. I can only feel my soul breaking under the thundering euphoria that racks my body. I'd scream out if Luther's cock didn't suffocate the sounds of my pleasure.

They take me so divinely. I crumble, and there's no putting me back together.

Trust Fall

"You need to rest," Jones says.

My head feels weightless, so I couldn't be more grateful for a break. It feels like I might pass out. Jones carefully unfastens the bindings around my wrists and ankles. He assists me off the saw horse. My joints ache, my muscles throb, and my vision swims. I've never had sex or orgasms that took so much out of me. It feels like I've just run a marathon.

"We'll meet you for dinner," Luther says as he caters to Monica. They walk out of the room before us.

Jones wraps my arm around his shoulder and supports my weight. His firm grip keeps me upright as we walk back to the room. I'm too out of it to concern myself with anything besides putting one foot in front of the other.

"You need to eat and sleep, but first, a bath before your muscles get too sore," he says.

"Okay," I say. He looks down at me with a concerned look as we walk. I fear he's questioning his decision to bring me here. I can't keep up, but I mask my exhaustion momentarily to add, "I don't need all that. Just a short break."

Jones's dark chuckle reverberates off the empty hallway. "You lie like a child, Kitten. You need rest. I don't consider it a weakness. I consider it a job well done on both our parts."

"Oh." A blush paints my cheeks. I don't know how this man can chastise and compliment me in one sentence and still make me want to please him.

He lifts my chin to face him as we walk down the dark hallway. "Don't be embarrassed, Kitten. You've done beautifully. I want to take care of you now." He plants a soft kiss on my forehead before releasing my chin.

Our steps are the only sound that accompanies us. Jones isn't much for words; frankly, I don't have enough energy to converse anyway. I might ask about tonight or tomorrow to mentally prepare myself if I did.

All my worries and questions are absolved by the exhaustion that weighs over me, though. Jones leads me to the bathtub, which he fills with steaming water and essential oils. He helps me sit in the water, then silently scrubs my skin with a luffa.

The rhythmic movement of his hands and the scratchy luffa achieve their intended purpose. My muscles no longer throb, and my vision is no longer hazy. The wound-up feeling in my gut subsides. The adrenaline finally fades.

"What do you want to ask, Kitten?" Jones says.

My eyebrows shoot up. The silence stretched so long that I nearly forgot he was here. "Um…Nothing," I say.

"You're a very poor liar. Do I need to explain this again?"

"No."

"This won't work if we aren't honest with each other. If you're curious about something, all you need to do is ask," Jones says.

"Okay…I guess I'm wondering what it takes to keep being your sub? I feel like I'm not going to pass the test."

Jones chuckles condescendingly. "I only keep one sub at a time, and you're doing beautifully. You're not even close to your full potential. We have plenty of time before you should be concerned about that."

"Does that mean you want to bring me back here?" I ask.

"Kitten, I have many plans for you. One of which includes bringing you back here next weekend." He pinches my chin, turning me to face him. "I'm going to use that pussy so thoroughly that you're going to beg for a weekend off. Do you understand me?"

I nod.

Jones massages my neck. He might not do flowers and wine, but he does neck massages. He said before that this relationship is about sex only. However, his caring behavior makes me doubt it.

I don't want to get emotionally tied down to an unavailable man. But I do want to come back here. I can't imagine anything more satisfying than begging for a weekend off. My pussy has never been used so thoroughly it needed a weekend off.

"Why are you taking care of me if our *relationship* is solely about pleasure?" I ask curiously.

"Because it's my job to ensure you are cared for physically and mentally. However, if you want more from me—something that ventures into a normal monogamous relationship—we'll have to end this arrangement. I can't give you that," Jones says matter-of-factly.

"I understand. I don't want a monogamous relationship right now anyway. I connected with you because I need this," I motion to my body and his. "I just want to make sure I understand how everything works because I've never done this before, and I can see how it might become complicated."

"I'm glad you're asking questions. And if you have more, I encourage you to ask them. I'm happy to clarify your concerns. The most important thing about this," Jones motions between our bodies as I did, "is that we're honest with each other and always communicate our needs."

"I can do that," I say.

It feels like a weight has been lifted off my shoulders. With things more clearly defined between Jones and me, I can relax knowing the sole purpose of our *relationship* is pleasure.

I need pleasure.

If this weekend has taught me anything, it's that I have a world of pleasurable experiences to explore. Jones is the perfect man to help me navigate the terrain. It's an equal partnership that allows us both to achieve our goals.

"Plus, it's my job as your dom to care for you. If I don't, you'll be useless later; our trust will break, and things will end badly. I enjoy making sure you're taken care of. I get hard thinking about being responsible for you—every part of you."

"Really?" I say, squeezing my thighs together. I never thought about how Jones might feel. I never considered that washing my hair and touching me gently might turn him on. I just thought he did it out of necessity or guilt.

"Is that so difficult to believe?" he asks.

I smile shyly, liking our open conversation. It makes me trust Jones more. Suddenly, I understand. There's a method to this madness.

"No. I guess I just never considered it. You're so dominant and rough with me normally. I didn't think you'd like this part," I say.

"Like I've said, you have much to learn but plenty of potential. Never assume, Kitten. Here," he says, taking my hand. He brings my palm to his crotch. He's rock-hard.

"Oh," I say as a blush heats my cheeks. This man is so damn sexy.

"Come on," he says, helping me stand. "Let's get some lotion on you."

I allow him to dry my body, then rub lotion into my skin while I stare at his cock straining against his pants. It feels nice to be taken care of like this, especially knowing how much the man doing the caretaking is enjoying himself.

There are no expectations for him to whisper pretty things in my ear. In fact, I only expect filthy things that make me horny to come out of his mouth. I like it that way. I want to keep it that way.

This sexual awakening has been a long time coming. I can't wait to see what Jones has in store for me tonight.

Kitten

"Time to go, Kitten," Jones says, smoothing my sleep-ridden hair. He took out my braids before my nap. It likely looks like a wild mane now.

The aching in my muscles has subsided, but a subtle tightness remains. I didn't sleep long. At this rate, I might be sleeping through the workweek to recover.

"What time is it?" I ask.

"It's nearly seven."

I sit up abruptly. "I slept the whole afternoon?"

"Yes, Kitten," Jones says, smirking. He's clearly satisfied with how much he's exhausted me, as if my exhaustion is a sign of a job well done.

"I need coffee," I say, knowing there's no way I'm going to make it through tonight without something to give me energy.

"You need food."

"Yes, that too," I say, accepting Jones's extended hand.

He effortlessly pulls me out of bed and leads me to the couch. My outfit is set out on the coffee table—if it can even be considered an outfit.

"What's this?" I say, lifting the edge of a heavy leather collar.

I recall the collar on that man's neck last night. This one is different, but there's no mistaking the leash attached to it.

"It's theme night, Kitten. You have to dress the part." Jones picks up the fuzzy headband. He holds it to my head, admiring the cat ears on it.

"Really?" I say while laughing. After everything we've done, dressing up as a sexy, naked cat is the last thing I would've expected to happen this weekend. I guess there's a reason he's been calling me Kitten. "When did you start planning this?" I ask.

He smirks. "You probably think I'm far more methodical than I am. I call you Kitten because that soft skin and pretty doe eyes nearly undid me the first time I saw you. But when I realized you've got sharp claws and teeth too, the pet name came easily."

"I don't have sharp claws and teeth," I say, running a finger along the edge of the furry ears.

"Ah. But you do. Underneath that sweet exterior is a hedonistic viper. Now that you've had a taste, you'll stop at nothing to get more."

I cross my arms. "That's not true."

"We'll see. Turn around," Jones says dismissively.

Instead of arguing, I turn. He runs his fingers through my hair, pulling it back before he slides the ears into place. With the headband on, my hair cascades down my back and off my face. I look at myself in the mirror and realize the waves created from my braids make it look like a lion's mane.

"I swear you planned this," I say.

"I guess you'll never know, Kitten. Now, get your knees," he says.

I glance at the remaining items and kneel before him. He secures the collar around my neck. It's not tight, but it's also not loose. The weight of it surprises me, though. It's solid, not some cheap, flimsy thing.

"Fuck. This is already turning me on, Kitten," Jones says huskily.

I try to hide my smile. I like knowing what turns him on. "What are the other things?" I ask, looking at the furry black cat tail and the long chain with six clamps.

"These are the finishing touches. This—" Jones picks up the tail "—goes in your ass."

"Oh," I say, feeling my breath catch as my sphincter clenches. "And those?"

"These," Jones lifts the thin chain and runs it through his fingers, "will be connected to the collar, your breasts, your sides, and your pussy."

My brows furrow, but I say, "Okay."

"Stand," Jones says.

Goosebumps break out along the back of my arms while my nipples harden in anticipation, remembering how those clamps made me feel. I wonder how long he'll make me wear them this time.

"So when do I put them on?" I ask.

Jones threads the chain through the collar. One end remains in his hand while the other side hangs between my breasts.

"First of all, I put them on, Kitten," he says.

He slowly picks up one clamp, rubbing the cold edge of the metal over my nipple. I suck in a breath as the sensation rolls down my spine. He opens the clamp and presses it into the flesh around my peaked tip.

"Ready?" Jones asks.

I take a deep breath, trying to calm my heart. My knees are already weak. I'm not sure I'll remain standing after he puts those on me.

"Yes," I manage to say.

The clamp closes around my nipple, and I let out a very kitten-like meowl. Jones is quick about the second one, not giving me a chance to get too worked up about it. The next clamp is just as firm and taunting. He takes two more clamps, securing them around the skin on my waist. The final two are secured on my labia.

He tugs at the chain, pulling everything skyward. The clamps hold tight while little pants of pleasure slip through my lips. When he loosens the leash and the clamps relax, I fall forward, gravity taking me down. Jones catches me and lowers me onto the floor. He situates me on all fours.

"Jones," I mutter.

He spanks me so hard that I almost topple face-first onto the carpet. "It's Daddy or sir," he says.

"I'm sorry, Daddy," I say, looking up at him with pleading eyes.

I'm soaked. I need him to fuck me already.

"Better. Now, for your tail," Jones says.

The chain clicks as I turn my head. The movement yanks at my nipples, sides, and labia once again, making my entire body sing. Jones runs a finger over my pussy.

"You're so wet. This will be easier than I thought. Just like before, Kitten. You can do it. I've been increasing the size every time," he says, coaching me.

He lifts the hard end of the tail, a cone-shaped object similar to the plugs. Replacing his finger with the silicon piece, he rubs it along my clit, enticing me more. He coats the plug in my desire, slipping the tip into me slightly.

I arch my back, permitting him to fuck me with it. But Jones moves further up, toward another entrance. Using the lubrication, he presses the tip into my backside.

"Breathe," Jones instructs.

I remember his teaching before and take a deep breath, bracing myself on my forearms with my ass arched high. The tip enters.

It's easier than last time. I can barely feel it. I rock my hips back, taking more of the plug into me. Now that I understand the sensation, I relax and take all of it into me.

"You learn quickly, Kitten. Look at you, taking my toys so easily. I should have got a bigger plug," Jones says.

I look back to see the tail, welcoming the sudden tingling stemming from my body as the chain pulls at the clamps again. "Is it in?"

"It's in. Feel this?" Jones asks, tugging on the end of the tail.

I gasp. My backside squeezes around the plug when he pulls at the tail, refusing to release as the thicker part nears the exit.

"Come look." He offers me a hand.

We walk to the floor-length mirror. The full outfit takes me aback. Despite my lack of makeup, my skin is glowing with that after-sex, thoroughly fucked look. My lips are swollen, and my cheeks are flushed. The silver chain is dainty and shiny against my skin, looking far sexier than I imagined it could. The black collar with matching cat ears and tail is darkly erotic, making my innocent side all but disappear behind this new sensual woman.

I feel as if my world has been flipped upside down. Before my nap, I felt awakened. But it wasn't until now that I see proof of that awakening. I'm embracing a part of myself that was never allowed to exist for fear that my desires were immoral and socially unacceptable.

But now.

I'm powerful. I'm a freaking goddess.

"What do you think, Kitten?" Jones whispers along my neck.

I lean back against him as he wraps his arms around my waist, one hand gliding down my abdomen, the other hand sliding up.

"I look amazing. I feel amazing," I say honestly.

He grabs the chain at my neck as his other hand finds my clit. "Just wait until tonight. You have no idea how amazing I'm going to make you feel," he says.

Watch Me

The chain slithers across my skin seductively. As we walk to the main room, other patrons stare conspiratorially in our direction. Little needs to be said under the weight of their gazes. Something is different about tonight.

Last night was libidinous, but tonight, a darkness taints the air. A hungry, near-desperate fascination has overtaken the warm bodies filling the Koala Club. It's as if everyone has waited their entire lives for tonight.

Granted, if I had known this world existed before, I might have the same yearning desire to be here.

I'm lucky. Jones brought me here without expectations, eliminating any preconceived notions I would've created before arriving. The lack of such stressful anticipation has made this entire event all the more satisfying.

My eyes have been opened, pinned back against my skull forcefully with my encouragement and permission. Jones is the best decision I've made in a while. Although, I'm not sure I can explain what happened this weekend to my friends without judgment. Some people wouldn't understand this relationship because they don't understand my needs.

There's a bond growing between Jones and me. It's a form of trust that's necessary for the sexual activities we partake in, but it's nothing more.

Emotionally—I trust Jones to take care of me like he has all weekend, but I don't rely on him to make me coffee and breakfast in the morning and ask about my day over dinner. This isn't a typical relationship, and the only people I'll be able to talk about it with are in this building.

I've tried to open up to past sexual partners and friends over the years. I wanted to discuss my desires and see if anyone else felt the same. But it ended as disastrously as a nuclear bomb exploding. This era is for me.

This time in my life is about *my* pleasure. *My* needs.

It's time for me to be selfish and explore my deepest, darkest fantasies, which I fully intend to do tonight. And I don't intend to explain myself or this new lifestyle to anyone but people who are willing to support or partake in it.

Jones and I settle into the same booth as last night. Although, unlike last night, the K-club has twice the occupancy. Every chair, couch, bed, cushion, and table in the room has been claimed, and every person is decked out in their finest erotic-themed wear.

Eyes scan the room, assessing, claiming, and engaging with others. People are looking for new and old partners. I notice the twins from last night. They wave at us before approaching a couple at a booth three down from Jones and me.

"We'll have more options tonight, Kitten. Keep your eyes open," Jones whispers.

I'm forced to lean forward in my seat due to the tail tucked into my behind. Jones comfortingly rubs my back as I lean into the table, eyes surveying the room.

"What about Luther and Monica?" I ask.

"Luther and Monica have some particular tastes they will be *digesting* tonight. But they'll come around later if that is what you want."

"I thought we were having dinner with them…" I wiggle my butt, and Jones chuckles.

"I love the enthusiasm, Kitten. I wanted you to rest, so they came to dinner earlier. Let's get some food in you," Jones says.

Jones orders grilled artichokes and steak while the performers take the stage. The show is similar to last night's performance but with more acrobatics thrown in the mix.

I make mental notes of the positions the women maneuver themselves into. They clearly practice with their partners. No words are exchanged, but they effortlessly flow into each position. I can't imagine how good it must feel to be so sexually attuned to someone else.

Similarly to last night, watching the performers while eating gets me worked up. Jones is content to rub my back, which helps me relax. I've nearly forgotten about all of the other people in the room. I'm consumed by the sensual comfort overwhelming my touch, taste, sight, and sound. Until Jones unzips his slacks, folding the flaps to the side and exposing his erection. He's not wearing any underwear. I arch my brow expectantly, waiting for instruction.

"Sit on my lap, Kitten," Jones says.

I slide onto his lap. My vulva pulses as soon as his cock touches it. Jones plants his hands on my hips and guides me, rocking my hips back and forth, rubbing me along his shaft.

The tail in my backside snags against him, moving around inside me as I grind on him, but the table presses into my upper thighs, limiting my movements. The limited room for motion has me aching for more.

Jones motions for a waitress, who rushes over at his beckoning.

"Yes, sir?" She says.

"Pull the table out a bit," Jones says.

Without even a glance at our bodies, she pulls the table out and walks away.

"Ride me," Jones whispers into my ear.

His husky voice grates against my nerves like a pumice scrubbing my skin clean. I lift off of him to reach between our bodies and grasp his penis. As I align his body with mine, I slowly sink down onto his cock.

Jones lets out a satisfied sigh. His hands flex against my thighs, but otherwise, they don't move, allowing me to take charge.

I buck my hips atop him, rolling my body and finding that sweet spot that is sure to make me scream.

"Do you see them watching?" Jones says.

I look up. People are watching us. With the table pulled back, I'm fully exposed. He wraps the leash around his hand and jerks it. The quick tug pulls the chain. The clamps tug upward, releasing a sharp sting to the chunk of skin each clasp holds. My inner walls clench around Jones's cock as the pain settles deliciously in my core.

"I asked you a question."

"Yes, Daddy," I say.

He twists the chain, then releases it, sending another wave of pain-laced pleasure down my body. I suck in an unsteady breath as his fingers dig into my hip.

"Don't you dare stop, Kitten. I want to hear you meow."

I roll my hips. Jones's shaft seems to grind against the butt plug inside me. The two objects fill my lower half and work with each other to heighten my pleasure.

"Let them hear you meow, Kitten. Now," Jones says.

I meow.

The hedonistic act sends me into overdrive. Jones plays with the chain as I lift myself off him and drop back onto him. The nips of pleasure pair perfectly with the full sensation of Jones and the plug. My body sings savagely as more people turn their eyes away from the performers to observe us.

The attention entices me.

I bounce on his cock faster, harder. A powerful emotion erupts within me.

The crude acts brings out a side of me that radiates with self-assurance. It overtakes my actions, and I begin to understand how the performers must feel on stage. Holding the audience's attention not only takes confidence but fosters it.

Even though I'm not a spectator, I know I'm glowing. I'm radiating. My glow is capturing everyone's attention, which makes me burn brighter. As the orgasm flows through me, I gyrate with a newfound sense of purpose.

The waves of pleasure paralyze my thoughts and steamroll my body. When it subsides, I fall back into Jones's chest, and he continues fucking me, letting our audience soak in the performance.

Showcase

"Let's go, Kitten. The show's over. It's time to play," Jones says.

Jones leads me through the room by the chain leash attached to my collar. The orgasmic haze weighs heavily on my eyelids. I struggle to process every face and body we pass. There are so many people, so much to take in and absorb.

Every shape, size, and skin color is in this room. It's like I'm at an all-you-can-fuck buffet. I thought this type of place only existed in Europe or, at least, the farthest part of the world from me, not in my city. Not that I'm complaining. I'm enamored. Entranced. I don't even have feelings or words for how thoroughly awed I am by this place.

We work our way around the edge of the room. There's a massive Alaskan king-size bed with two women lying across it as three giant pythons slither across them. My mouth drops open as I watch the women lazily touch the silky scales without flinching as the snake heads near their faces. The women and pythons seem perfectly happy lying around and soaking in the abundant venereal energy.

Another section of the room is lined with carabiners and ropes. Men and women are tied up with intricate knots pressing into their skin. Some rope is rough, while others look more like silk. I rub my upper arms as I regard a man with a frayed rope tied so tightly around his arms that he has to be getting a burn.

Jones continues to pull me along, letting me stop to watch occasionally. There's so much going on here that I'm unsure where I want to begin. Watching is enough to make me wet. Yet, my curiosity keeps me from staying in one spot too long until Jones stops me in the middle of the floor.

"Take your pick," he says.

"My pick of what?" I ask.

"Of anything, Kitten. Show me what you want. There's something here for everyone—whether it's a person or experience."

Once again, Jones empowers me to make the choice. Initially, I thought a sub held no power, but the further into this relationship we get, the more power I realize I have.

"I want…I want to be right here," I say.

"In the middle? So you want people to watch us?" he asks.

"Yes."

There isn't exactly space on the furniture for us. Every square inch of the place is covered in primarily naked bodies, drinking, kissing, fucking. Not that it would stop me. Something about how everyone's attention turned to Jones and I fucking at the table changed me. I want to prove what else I can do and how good I can make him feel.

"Okay," Jones says. He loosens the chain, letting it drop between my breasts. "Do you see anyone that you want to join us?" He drags a finger across my collarbone, stopping to turn my face left. Jones leans in and whispers as I regard potential partners, not just onlookers, for what we're about to do. "Tell me, Kitten. Does anyone catch your eye?"

Many people attract my attention, but one in particular makes my stomach clench. A tall man with dark skin and a shaved head. His teeth gleam from the other side of the room as he smiles at me. I can't help but feel like those sensual curved lips and narrow eyes have been watching me for a while. My intrigue peaks. He's gorgeous and intense. I immediately find myself wanting to know more.

"Him," I say, pointing.

The man starts walking toward us. Jones spins me around so my front faces the stranger approaching us. He presses into my back, wrapping an arm tightly around my waist. The pressure shifts the chain running down my body, tugging the clamps around, which only fuels my desire.

"What do you want him to do, Kitten?" Jones asks.

"I don't know," I say, realizing I have no idea what I want other than to feel good and prove myself to Jones.

"Do you want him to taste you?"

My stomach knots. The man is getting closer, nearly within hearing range. "Maybe," I say.

"Do you want him to fuck you?" Jones says.

The bald man wearing nothing but boxer briefs stops before us, close enough to hear my reply. "Maybe," I say.

The stranger's voice is a deep, slow vibrato that makes my groin ache. "Hello, beautiful. Are you looking to play tonight?"

"She is," Jones answers for me.

"Call me Adonis," the stranger says.

Jones stifles a laugh before saying, "Fitting, Adonis. If you can make her purr, you can fuck her."

"Excuse me?" I thought the *purring* was reserved for our play.

"I can't let just anyone fuck you, Kitten. They need to earn it. Let's see if Adonis knows how to make a woman purr."

Jones is playing into my cat outfit tonight, and I like it. I've never been into bestiality, but wearing this tail and these ears while he calls me *Kitten* makes my skin tingle.

"I'll do more than that, Jones," Adonis says.

A look of shock paints my face, making both men laugh devilishly. "You know each other?" I ask.

"I know all the regulars, Kitten," Jones says condescendingly.

It occurs to me that as much power as I might hold, Jones will always have the upper hand here. So far, his power has been to my advantage—he's only made me feel safe while being pleasured beyond my wildest dreams. If he knows everyone here, he knows their abilities, their limits. He knows who will satisfy me the most.

"You already know how he'll make me feel," I say. It's a statement, not a question.

"I do," Jones says.

"Then why put a stipulation on it?"

"Because Jones wants to make sure I'm not lazy with you, pretty girl. He's making sure you're properly taken care of. After all, that's his job," Adonis says.

I return my attention to Jones as he slides the chain through his fingers. He gently tugs on the end, pulling my clamped skin skyward. It makes my body seize.

"Such a pretty girl," Adonis says. My skin crawls at the sound of his voice.

Jones places his hands on my hips, kneading my sides. I push my ass into his groin, but his fingers dig in—warning me to keep my attention focused elsewhere.

Adonis leans in, planting a soft kiss on my shoulder. His bald head moves downward, peppering lush kisses along the delicate parts of my frame. When he reaches my side, he nips the skin. And when I jump, Adonis bites my side again.

A surge of heat shoots straight into my core with each slight pinch. He nips my belly and sticks his tongue into my belly button. Adonis explores the tiny hole, showing me how he might explore other holes.

At the same time, Jones's teeth clamp down on my ear, distracting me. He sucks in my lobe, rolling it between his teeth.

The two men are hitting every erogenous zone, making me drunk with lust.

Adonis veers south as he grabs my buttcheeks and spreads them apart. The plug fights to stay put, forcing my entire lower body to clench as Adonis sucks my clit into his mouth.

I cry out as soon as his tongue flicks around the sensitive bud of nerves. My head falls back onto Jones's shoulder. He fully supports my upper body as Adonis savagely eats me out, and I struggle to remain standing.

His fingers dig painfully into my backside, forcing my body to remain clenched around the plug as his mouth engulfs me. His wide tongue grinds into my center while the tip of his teeth bites into my mons pubis.

Jones plunges his tongue into my ear, sensually assaulting my hearing.

"I have a surprise for you, Kitten. Remember to trust me," he says. His hands release for a moment, but I'm distracted by the god of a man below me whose shoulders I use for support.

Adonis releases my butt. My entire body relaxes, and then a sharp stinging slap lands across my clit, and I explode.

A purr doesn't even touch what escapes my lips. I roar. But I'm not given much opportunity to think about the sounds coming out of my mouth because my senses are stupified by the licentious pleasure being delivered by Jones and Adonis.

It doesn't stop there, though. Jones grabs my face, yanking my head back as clear plastic wrap is wound around my face.

I take a breath but suck in the cling wrap. The last bit of oxygen between my skin and the wrap burns down my throat.

The air grows hot and sticky. Panic consumes me. I reach up to rip it off, but Jones pins my arms behind my back.

"Tap twice for red," he says, giving me another way to signal in case it's too much. He shifts my arms so I can tap on his, but he keeps them pinned.

I don't tap. Not yet.

But I'm unable to stop my body's bucking reaction when the air is taken from me. I suffocate in the plastic wrap as it sucks into my mouth and tightly forms around the contours of my face. I can barely manage a blink. And I'm nearly too scared to do so, as it might be the last time my eyes close.

The pain from the clamps becomes unbearable, intensifying as my breathing slows. It's at such odds with the type of debilitating pleasure owning my lower body.

But Jones doesn't let go of my arms, and Adonis doesn't stop eating me out.

Sweat glides down my body as I choke. My vision blurs, cutting in and out, but Adonis keeps going. His tongue plunges into my pussy, sliding up my folds.

My knees buckle, and Adonis lifts my legs over his shoulders. Jones's arms are under mine. I sag against them, entirely at their mercy. My last breath is gone. I can't hold out any longer. I'm going to die like this—mounted between two men who control and devour me.

Adonis sinks his digits into my center as his cheeks hollow, sucking in my clit. His tongue flicks across my clit as his fingers curl and thrust inside me. I shake involuntarily, on the cusp of passing out, when two fingers tear the plastic wrap over my mouth. Air rushes in—cold and fiery all at once. I gasp just as the orgasm takes me.

A cry so feral that I don't recognize myself rips out of me. It feels as if time and space have halted. I'm suspended in the air. My body is of its own mind. And then there's nothing.

Wet Spread

J ones leads me to a plush couch, lowering me onto it slowly. My ears ring, cutting off all other sounds in the pleasure den. I feel thoroughly fucked. But I haven't even been fucked yet.

"You doing okay, Kitten?" Jones asks, lifting my chin. His eyes scan my face as if searching for signs of harm.

"I'm okay," I mumble.

I passed out. I've never passed out after something like that before. Of course, I've also never done anything like that before. Part of me thinks it was from the lack of oxygen, but I don't think that was the only reason. The plastic wrap wasn't on me for very long. It was the combination—the asphyxiation and the orgasm.

He grins. "Do you want to return to the room for the night?"

My body sinks into the cushions, but I say, "No."

"Can I trust you to know your limits, Kitten?" Jones fears I don't know when I've had too much. Passing out probably scared him. After all, it was a direct result of his *surprise*.

"Yes," I say. "Red. Yellow. Green. I remember."

It feels like I've been drinking too much—on the edge of knowing I'll have a hangover tomorrow but too close to that wonderful feeling that makes me not want to stop. I'll definitely be exhausted and sore. However, I know how good Jones makes me feel, and I want to know what else he has in store for me tonight.

"I liked it. I'd do it again. Well, maybe not right away. I need a break, but I would be willing to try something like that again," I add.

Finally, he nods, trusting me to know my limits. Curiosity and the promise of pleasure have been carrying me through this weekend, and they will carry me through until the end, regardless of how tired I feel tonight.

"I need some water," I say.

"Stay here," Jones says. He disappears into the crowd but returns with water and massage oil moments later. "Here." He hands me the water.

I down the entire glass. I never thought sex could make me so thirsty, but my prior sex life isn't anything compared to what I've experienced this weekend. In fact, I barely even notice I'm naked anymore. Everyone around me is half-clothed or less. It feels natural to be baring my body shamelessly.

Jones pours oil onto his hand and begins working it into my neck. His hands move expertly down my back, digging into the muscles around my hips. His touch grounds me, making the lightheadedness disappear.

"There are a few options for us tonight, Kitten. I'd like you to pick one," Jones says.

"What options?"

"As far as what type of play you want to partake in," Jones explains. "We can stay in the main room and continue playing with others or go to a private room. You've had a taste of both. Which do you prefer?"

"I like it out here," I say, looking at our lascivious surroundings. "But I like it in the room too…When Luther and Monica joined us—that was fun."

"Let's start here. Luther and Monica will be around eventually," Jones suggests.

I touch my backside, expecting to find my cell phone in a back pocket, but realize I haven't thought twice about my phone this weekend. I wonder how he's keeping tabs on Luther and Monica.

Granted, Jones is always dressed, so he probably has a pocket to keep it in. If they even allow that type of thing here. I haven't seen anyone with a phone or camera. Not that I'm complaining. I'm glad no one is filming me.

The K-club is a place where the things you do might not be accepted in the social circle you frequent outside. I can't imagine what my brother might say. He invited me to move out here. I don't think he expected me to do something like this, but he travels so often that he'll never find out what I'm up to.

I much prefer to keep it that way. This is for me.

"Okay," I say. "So where do we start?"

"Let's ease into it, Kitten. Stay put."

Jones leaves me on the couch with an empty water glass. I'm basically thirsting—and not just for water—as I see him turn his attention to the room.

By the tone of his voice, staying put isn't an option—unless I want to be punished. He wants me to rest. His concern is cute and probably warranted, so I listen to him even though a punishment doesn't sound too bad.

He crosses the space we occupied with Adonis, who's on his knees, sucking someone's cock. People move on quickly here. I'm torn between watching him and Jones, but decide I better pay attention to my dom.

Jones approaches a group of incredibly fit women. They seem more content with keeping to themselves—enjoying each other's company and bodies. But as soon as Jones enters their invisible bubble of privacy, two of the women part, allowing him to sit between them.

His mouth is moving, but from my vantage point, I have no idea what he's saying.

The women are mesmerized by him. I can't blame them. His jawline is like a damn sculpture. All five sets of eyes gleam brightly with the promise of fucking him. Usually, I'd be jealous of someone looking at my man that way, but Jones isn't *my* man. And it doesn't take long for five sets of eyes to set their sights on me.

I give a shy wave, unsure if Jones is propositioning them or doing something else entirely. Jones and the K-club are still a mystery to me. They're a compelling force that draws me in one orgasm at a time, but the underlying promise of something dark and dangerous lingers.

The two women who sit on either side of Jones turn their attention back to him. Their hands slide up the inside of his thighs. One of them cups him while the other slowly unbuttons his dress shirt.

Jones leans back into the couch cushions, letting them do all the work. A third woman leans over him from behind and kisses his lips. Soon, all five women's hands and eyes are on Jones, undressing him.

A hostess walks by, retrieving his clothing. She folds them neatly, resting them over one arm before walking off. The mystery of where everyone's clothing goes is solved, but Jones's current ploy is not.

His eyes lock with mine as he pushes the woman at his face down to his neck, allowing her to pepper kisses along his stubbly jawline so he can watch me watching him.

A fourth woman is on her knees in front of him. She pulls down his briefs, revealing his cock. Something inside me twitches.

When her mouth surrounds the head of his cock, my lips part. They become dry with my heavy breaths.

She deep throats him, and the memory of his cock jammed down my throat makes me suck in a breath with her. He places his hand on the back of her head, holding her down while he grins at me. When she pulls away, her mouth drips saliva onto his cock.

Jones's grin is wicked.

He's across the room, yet he still manages to make me…feel. His actions pull me to the edge of my seat, heating the blood under my skin. There's an itch inside me, and its intensity grows as I watch him.

The fifth woman, who has been taking a back seat to the event, walks around the couch to face Jones. Her shiny black hair skims an impossibly tiny waist.

I can't see her face, but her body is flawless. There isn't a dimple or curve in sight that God himself didn't place on her. She's beautiful. And I find myself a tidge jealous that she's standing in front of Jones and not me. She blocks my view of him as she straddles his hips.

Even from this far away, I can see her arousal when the light shines on her cunt. She rubs herself along Jones's shaft. His hands grab her waist, guiding her. He pulls her down and whispers something in her ear. He's still looking at me as he speaks to her though.

The beautiful woman turns her head to stare at me, too. She lifts a dainty, manicured finger and motions me over.

My feet have never moved faster. I cross the room and stop abruptly, awkwardly standing behind them.

"Stand behind her. Guide her, Kitten. Show her how to fuck my cock," Jones says.

My entire body clenches as his intentions become clear. This dom–sub dynamic is still foreign to me. The amount of control Jones gives me doesn't make me feel like a submissive, but I trust him to know the roles.

I take hold of her hips and steer her body to align with Jones. I reach between them with one hand, holding his cock upright, while my other hand pinches the woman's side in a command to lower herself.

She does.

Keeping my hand on Jones's shaft, the woman's sex sinks down, pressing against my hand. I grip him tighter, straining to *feel* the same tightness the woman is feeling as he fills her.

"You're not doing a very good job showing her, Kitten," Jones says.

I release him. "Sorry," I say quietly, placing my hands on the woman's impeccable backside and wanting to do a better job.

I dig my fingers into the firm mounds of her ass, spreading her butt cheeks apart and tugging her up. I steer her hips, teaching her how to ride Jones. The sensual sounds of lust pour from her perfectly pouty lips. Jones's face is stern as he watches me. He's not pleased, but I don't know why.

"Turn around," I tell the woman.

She spins around, releasing Jones's cock only for a moment. With her legs spread on either side of his, I pin my hands below her thighs, helping her bounce on top of him.

Jones's long fingers snake up her sides, palming her breasts as he pulls her into his chest. She falls backward. The movement traps my hands and pulls me forward. My face is inches from their lower bodies as Jones starts thrusting into her.

"Eat her pussy, Kitten. You should know how to do it now," Jones says.

My lower body aches as his words resonate within me. I'm so close to their conjoined bodies that the woman's arousal sprinkles my face as Jones fucks her. I want to please him, though. I want to make sure he doesn't regret bringing me here so I lean in, my heart racing as I approach her sex. Shyly, I lick up the center of her body. She moans.

"That's it, Kitten. Play along, clean her pussy," Jones says.

I lick her again, tasting something sweet and salty. Her hips rock forward, asking for more. Jones slows his thrusts so her body doesn't move as much as I press my lips against her clit and open my mouth. My tongue darts out and tastes her again, feeling the grooves of her lower body as I search for the spot that aches on my own body.

I find it and focus on it.

The woman pants above me, reaching for my head and weaving her fingers into my hair. She holds me down as I suck in the tip of her clitoris. She cries out for more. My body frantically hums with the same craving need to be touched and sucked, but I keep my attention on my task.

"Be a bad kitty and bite her now, Kitten," Jones commands.

I do what he says. I nip her clit, and she cries out. Jones thrusts into her two more times, and then liquid explodes out of her body, straight into my mouth, and onto my face.

"Ravish her," Jones growls.

I do. I open my mouth and do what can only be described as ravishing while she squirts into my mouth. My mind shuts off as my body follows Jones's commands, and I make this woman scream. She cums so hard I'm both proud and jealous when it finally ends.

Jones lets out a shallow grunt, pushes the woman off of him, and cums into the air. Tiny beads of his seed hit my chest. "My perfect little pet. You look beautiful with my cum on your tits," he says as he finishes, his focus solely on me.

Fucking her wasn't for him. It was for me to see that he needs me just as much as I need him. That his pleasure is my pleasure. That my service is his service.

The women take their leave—kissing Jones in thanks. I hadn't even paid attention to what the others were doing, but apparently, they had fun, too. The woman, whose lower body I had just become well acquainted with, languidly kisses me in thanks, too.

"I hope we see each other again," she whispers as they leave.

Pussy Cats

"Stay on your knees, Kitten," Jones says. He picks up the chain leash hanging slack between my breasts. "Follow me." I start to stand, but a firm hand lands on my shoulder, pushing me down. "I said stay on your knees," Jones says.

"What am I supposed to do—crawl?" I ask.

A smirk lifts one side of Jones's thin lips. There's a fire in his eyes. He looks as excited by the prospect of me refusing him as he is by my following his command. I choose obedience over punishment—because I want to see where this is going—as I place my palms against the floor.

"That's a good pet," Jones says.

He leads me along the wall, weaving between people who narrowly miss stepping on my fingers. But when they notice me, their eyes change. Some are intrigued. Some are dismissive. If I'm not mistaken, some are jealous.

I'm not sure how to feel about this type of play. I'm a *kitten* on a leash. It feels disparaging, but it also feels invigorating because I'm not being ostracized for my actions. Fully participating in the kink is celebrated here. It's like being part of a secret club.

We stop beside a metal cage with a man inside. I give Jones a knowing look.

"Play along and be a good pet, Kitten."

"In there?" I point to the occupied cage. The man has hair like a lion's mane, and his golden skin is rippled with muscles like one, too. I've never seen a more dangerously beautiful man.

"Yes. Tiffany, would you mind if I put my pet in the cage with yours?" Jones asks someone.

Their face is out of range from my vantage point on the floor, but the reply is clear and sharp. "He's being wild tonight. I brought him in for breeding. Tread lightly."

"Ah. Breeding…" Jones strokes his chin in consideration, then kneels beside me. "Her pet is going to fuck you. He won't be wearing a condom, and he'll come inside you. That's part of the whole breeding thing. Do you understand?"

"I understand, but I thought only you come in my pussy," I say.

"This is different. I'm allowing it because I like to watch two caged animals fuck. Now, are you going to please Daddy and get in there? Or do I need to stuff you in a cage and make you watch someone else lick up my cum?"

My heart beats wildly. Both are good options, but I realize I want his cum. I don't want to share it tonight. He can share me, but his cum is my cum.

"I want to be bred, Daddy," I say, giving him a sultry look.

Jones is pleased. "Remember to use your words," he reminds me.

He's going to put me in there. I don't know what's come over me but I can't wait. My thighs press together in anticipation. My pussy is soaked from our exploits earlier. I remember the words, but after looking at the man in the cage, I won't need them. I want him to press me against the bars of the cage and have his way with me.

"I'll use them if I need, Daddy," I reassure Jones.

He unhooks the chain and removes the clamps. My body throbs when they are finally released. I was beginning to get used to them, but now that they are gone, I have a whole new sensation running through me. The pinched skin is sensitive to everything, even the air. My nipples especially. They ache and throb just as insistently as my pussy.

Jones opens the cage door and I crawl in. The man, who looks like a lion, sits on his heels, patiently waiting for the door to close. As soon as the lock slides into place, he barrels across the cage, knocking me onto my back.

He sprawls across me, running his nose along my side. His hair tickles my belly, making me squirm. The lion man takes note and pins my legs with his own so I can't get away. His knees dig into my thighs. He's not gentle.

"I smell you," he says. He nuzzles me. The broad width of his tongue slides up the base of my neck. "I taste you," he growls.

The man pushes his hips into me. His erection juts into my center but doesn't enter. It presses into the area between my holes, stabbing me. I tilt my hips, welcoming him to take me, but he pulls back before he can slip inside me. I groan.

His lips graze my ear as he whispers, "Do you want to play, little cat?"

It seems even between the submissives, permission must be given.

"Yes," I say, practically begging.

The opening of his mouth and the press of his teeth along the outside of my ear tell me all I need to know about how pleased he is by my answer. And before I can roll my head to face him, his cock is shoving into me. He grunts his approval as his pelvis hits mine.

I exhale loudly as my body is finally touched in the spot that has been aching all evening. The lion man rolls his hips hypnotically, languidly. He bites my shoulder as his approach to taking me turns animalistic.

He pulls up my legs, pinning them beside my waist as he rears back and watches his body enter mine. His golden hair falls around his face, making him appear nearly feral. But he maintains control, slowing down his thrusts, teasing me with his cock. He retracts until the head of his cock barely rests inside me, leaving me desperate and clenching.

"Please," I beg him for more.

The man slowly pushes back into me, all the way to the hilt. He does something with his hips that forces the tip of his penis to prod at my G-spot. Slowly, so slowly, he takes me. And every time his cock touches that spot, my body shakes.

A low, guttural growl trembles across his lips. I feel his cock swelling inside me.

"Not yet," I beg, needing my release too.

He leans down, pressing his chest onto the back of my thighs, stretching me so he can touch the deepest part of my cunt. My legs brush against my aching nipples, making me cry out from the pain. Everything is so sensitive, so heightened.

"Come with me, or don't come at all," he says threateningly.

Then he slams into me. His cock plunges into my pussy.

The slow taunt has me burning, but this change in pace and aggression lights a fuse. My pussy suffocates his cock, refusing to let him withdraw as it clenches around his shaft with a dire need to be filled.

He carries on, fucking me aggressively, not giving me an ounce of control. His hands bind my ankles above my head as his lower body pounds into mine, making my body rock. The momentum makes every thrust feel more brutal than the last, letting him go deeper.

As soon as the heat of his semen blows inside me, I find my release, too. My body sucks him in, clamping down around his bulging cock. His arousal mixes with mine. The scent of sex and sweat is heavy in the air as I feel our combined cum forcefully spurting out of my pussy.

The sticky substance coats my lower body as the man slowly lets go of my legs. He nuzzles into me again, gentler than before, but he doesn't remove himself.

"Are you going to pull out?" I ask.

He smirks and licks the sweat off my neck. "No, little cat. I'm going to fuck my cum into you. Then, I'm going to fill you again. I'm going to put little pussy cats in you," he says.

My skin reignites, burning from his sensual promise.

Bad Behavior

"That's enough," Jones says, opening the cage door and motioning me forward. The lion man has his arms wrapped firmly around my chest. He growls at Jones, who returns a smirk. "Tiffany, mind your pet," Jones says threateningly.

Tiffany picks up a leather cord and wacks it across the ground. The moment the sound snaps across the room, the man releases me. I scramble away from him and toward Jones. But a tug at my backside stops me.

I rear back to find my tail in the lion man's mouth. He pulls, and I shift back, trying not to let the plug come out while a moan escapes me. I almost forgot it was back there.

"Naughty cat," Tiffany hisses.

He bares his teeth as he tugs on my tail, making my ass clench. I scoot back to avoid losing the plug. It feels too tempting to have it jostled back and forth in this power match between two doms and a misbehaving sub. I'm stuck in the middle of something I'm not sure I can handle.

"Use your words, Kitten, and we will proceed accordingly," Jones says. It feels like a coaching moment.

The man behind me tugs at my tail again, pulling me backward. My lips form the words, but I don't say anything for some reason. Jones eyes me suspiciously. He places a hand on Tiffany's shoulder as she raises the whip, ready to crack it across the cage in warning.

"It seems my pet wants to keep playing, Tiffany. I deprived her yesterday. Let them enjoy themselves," Jones says.

"You never let your subs have this much power, Jones. Did you find a magical pussy? If so, I want to try." Tiffany eyes me seductively.

"Save it for another weekend. This is new for her. She needs to figure out her boundaries. Let your cat show her a thing or two," Jones replies.

His remark replays in my mind, but I don't make much sense of it. I'm trying to figure out my boundaries. At this point, I'm not sure there are any we will come across this weekend. I simply want to feel good. And being in this cage with this sensually beautiful man, acting like an animal, is too fucking hot to stop. Especially after he promised to fuck the cum leaking between my legs back into me. I never had a breeding kink before, but damn if I don't now.

A low, threatening rumble reverberates through his chest as he tugs one final time on my tail as if to tell me to pay attention to him. I fall back into his lap, and his cock bounces against my bare pussy. It glistens with my cum.

He lifts us onto our knees, positioning himself at my center as his fingers stitch around my sides, digging into me painfully.

I whimper.

"My kitty," he says possessively, too quiet for anyone but me to hear.

I'm beginning to think this *cat* doesn't play well as a submissive—or at least, what I believe is expected from a submissive. My knowledge of the roles is based on pornography and books that never delve too deep into the subject. The reality is far from my fantasy. It's more satisfying and more terrifying.

His cock rubs between my legs, teasing me. He wants to work me up.

"Be a good kitty," I say, my only warning.

He places his cheek on my shoulder, licking the side of my neck slowly as if he's cleaning me. His whisper hisses past my ear. "My kitty. My kitty. *My* kitty."

Then, his hand reaches between our bodies, and he aligns himself with me. I'm ready for him. I'm so wet it's impossible for him not to slip into me.

His shaft glides across my inner walls. It feels so easy taking him. He's not as thick or long as Jones, but it still feels amazing.

My head falls back onto his shoulder as I allow him to take me again. He slowly rolls his hips while his mouth opens against my neck. His tongue slides across my jugular, wetting my skin, before he clamps down. His teeth bite into me, forcing a shrieking cry of pain out of my lips.

My entire body knots, seizing up as he forces his teeth to pierce my skin. His lips wrap around them, and his tongue slips through. The force of his thrusts match the intensity of his bite and the strength of my roar.

He slaps my breast, switching between them and delivering sharp, stinging blows. The sound rings against my ears as he does it repeatedly, making my body red under his hand. His teeth hold me down, forcing my body to remain tense so he doesn't bite me any harder. My body shakes from an overdose of endorphins and adrenaline.

The cat man releases my neck, and I fall forward, away from him, but he follows me down.

His weight pins me to the floor. His hands press into my back as his thighs force my legs closed. At this angle, his cock feels monstrous as it enters me.

I arch my back, and he takes it as a challenge, plunging harder into me.

Wetness coats my cheeks as he wraps a hand around my hair, pulling it back and pushing my face into the ground at the same time. I cry out, trying to tear out of his grasp, but he collapses on top of me, hands holding mine flat against the cold cage floor.

"*My kitty*," he growls.

My nails scrape the ground, trying to hold onto something as the weight of his body takes the breath from my lungs, and the strength of his thrusts makes my skin scratch against the floor. It's so primal. Yet, I love it. The only word I want to scream is *green*.

He vigorously takes me as everyone outside the cage bares witness to our primitive behavior. We've descended to our base instincts, lost in pain and pleasure—the two things that make us feel more than anything else in life can.

All I manage to get out is an *umph* when his teeth bite into my upper trap, and my body transcends.

The heat resonating between our skin turns celestial, and I swear we both enter a new realm of the universe. It's as if I'm experiencing a spiritual rebirth—a sensual rebirth.

My vision blacks out, and my mind swims through hallucinatory, colorful blobs of light.

"*My kitty*," he says again as he drowns my pussy in cum.

Light Switch

"Come now, Kitten," Jones says, stroking my hair out of my face.

I wake up on a couch in one of the private rooms. "What happened?" I lift my head, but it spins, forcing me to fall back onto Jones's lap.

"You passed out when the little cat was fucking you. Tiffany's punishing him now." He's so matter-of-fact.

"Punishing him—how?" I ask.

Jones shushes me. "He's getting exactly what he wanted. I'm certain he'd love to have you assist in the punishing. Is that something you'd like to help with, Kitten?" Jones's tone is carefully inquisitive.

"No," I say honestly. I don't want to punish anyone. The only type of punishment I enjoy is the playful kind Jones has been delivering me all weekend.

"Good," he says satisfactorily. "You've done so well this weekend. I want to reward you."

He strokes a knuckle down my cheek, then scrapes his nail on the underside of my jaw. I lift my chin to avoid the sharp graze, which is probably exactly what he wants me to do. It places me eye to eye with him, but still below as I remain sprawled across his lap.

"What's my reward?" I ask.

"I think you know," he says. His eyes flicker between my legs as his hand shifts from my hip to the crease between my abdomen and thigh.

Two men. Two men taking *me* is the reward.

The prospect has me clenching, which is when I realize the plug is gone. I look down to find myself stripped bare. No accessories or adornments. It's just my body. And something about being in the nude without an outfit to intensify my pleasure and emphasize my body parts makes this even more intimate and exciting.

Not to mention, knowing Jones removed the sex toys and lingerie while I was passed out is darkly erotic. I probably shouldn't get off on the idea of him touching my body while I'm unconscious, but that hidden part of me Jones brought to the surface this weekend basks in the idea of him doing whatever he wants to me, even when I'm unable to say no.

"With Luther?" I ask.

"Yes. He and Monica are finishing up their session. We'll let him know we're ready as we head back to the room," Jones says.

"What room?"

"The room you've slept in all weekend, Kitten. I want you to relax for your first time doing anal. It's overwhelming enough on its own, and you've exhausted a lot of energy this weekend."

Fair enough. My limbs do feel heavier than usual, and soreness is setting into my muscles. I'll be paying for this weekend over the next week.

"Okay," I say.

When my dizziness subsides enough to leave the strangely quiet dungeon room Jones ascertained after I passed out, he leads me to our final destination. We walk down the familiar dark hallways, passing door after door. Mysterious sounds filter through the tiny crack underneath each.

Jones pauses at a door labeled with the number nine. He knocks three times, pausing between each thump.

Luther opens the door halfway but quickly blocks my view inside by moving into the open-door jam. I briefly glimpse a tattooed arm pinned against a medieval-looking device.

Jones steps in front of me, blocking the remainder of my view as he and Luther exchange hushed words. I'm too busy imagining what Luther and Monica are up to in that room to pay attention to what they say. But the door soon shuts, and Jones continues leading me back to my accommodations.

He opens the door with a key card. The room is exactly as we left it. The only change from earlier is a freshly made bed, courtesy of housekeeping.

Jones walks me through the small sitting area toward the bed. He motions for me to lie down. "We can stop the act for now, Kitten," he says.

"What do you mean?"

Jones sits down on the bed beside me. He leans on one shoulder casually. "We don't need to play into any dom or sub roles for this. You've performed well above expectations. Let me pleasure you in a more simplistic fashion. Let me and Luther give you… Give you something as close to normal—as we know it—as possible. This world will bring you more satisfaction than you've ever imagined, but it's important for *you* to enjoy normal sexual behavior as well."

After the weekend I've just had, I don't think normal can ever compare. Nor do I understand why Jones, who was quite clear on his intentions and expectations, wants me to experience *normal* with him.

"Why are you saying this? I don't get it. I like what's happened this weekend. I love it," I say, exacerbated.

He lets out a half laugh, half sigh. "Kitten, you won't be my sub forever. You aren't the type to be anyone's submissive for too long."

My brows furrow, mulling over how different his words are from this past weekend. "Am I not doing a good job?" I ask. He lifts my chin. I hadn't even realized I looked away.

"You've done spectacularly. But you aren't meant to be a sub," he says.

"Why do you say that?" My heart aches as fear takes a tight hold on me. This place is amazing. It's all I've ever dreamed of experiencing.

I cross my arms over my chest, suddenly feeling exposed. Jones undoes them, holding them to the side and shamelessly eye fucking my body. No matter how insecure and confused I suddenly feel, the want in his eyes makes me desire his touch, so I don't fight back. I wish I could slap him for promising me pleasure beyond my wildest dreams this weekend and now taking it all back.

"I'm telling you this because it's true, Lily."

My breath catches when he uses my name. Jones has never used my name.

He continues, "Don't take this the wrong way. I want to keep our relationship going, and we will. But eventually, you'll outgrow my needs and develop more of your own. You deserve everything you want, and I'm not greedy enough to hold you back when the time comes to let you go. Also, I have some more particular tastes that I know you wouldn't be well suited for. You'd be more of a brat than a true submissive, which is fine, but it won't fulfill that need for me."

"Oh," I say. It's unexpected. I haven't been thinking about much past all the pleasure I've been experiencing, but I find my trust in Jones growing as he considers my future needs. "Are you trying to say I'm not a submissive?"

"I believe you'll likely become a switch and then a dom in your own right. Many of us take time to develop. I started as a submissive. It's important to understand all roles in order to play safely, so this is a good start for you. I'll help you as much as I can, and when you're ready to take on a more dominant role, I'll connect you with other partners—if you wish."

"Okay…" Again, I consider his words. "I can't imagine myself as a dom. I like you taking the lead, and I don't understand how this plays into you giving me something *normal*, as you say, when it's been clear from the start that this relationship is only about sex," I say.

"Luther and I have fairly normal appearing relationships in the outside world. We also have less commonly known types of relationships that we maintain on the side. Here. But we get a taste for romance, monogamy, and all that jazz in part of our lives. You're young. You still have time to develop both your sexual desires and healthy emotional relationships. Doing something a bit more vanilla—mind you, anal is more like vanilla chocolate chip to most people—will keep the new experiences exciting for longer."

"I get that, but I'm loving all this new stuff… It's enlightening. In the best way!" I explain.

"Good. It should be, but let's take it slow, or you'll move on from me too fast," Jones says with a sultry wink.

I bite my lower lip, wanting to push back, but he's right. The lust is riding me, making me reach for the next best, most insane physical act I can experience. Passing out should be a solid enough caution sign.

"Thank you for watching out for me," I say, truly meaning it.

"Always, Kitten," Jones says with finality. "I have dirty martinis on the way. In the meantime, let's dance."

He pops up from the bed and starts setting the mood, turning on music and lighting candles. It's cute, but I remind myself that it's only temporary.

Jones is still playing his role as a dom by taking care of me. If that means taking it slow and giving me more tame experiences, that's what he'll do. Because he wants to keep me for as long as he can.

And while that doesn't pull at my heartstrings, making me fall in love, it does soothe me. He makes me feel comfortable and safe. I can see how people would start to want more from him. Fortunately, I have a lot more love to take before I'm ready to give.

"I didn't expect you to be such a romantic," I tease.

Jones's personality turns from stoic under lord to easygoing frat boy as he presses play on the controller and shimmies his shoulders to a new beat.

"We're just dancing, Kitten. Don't tell me you can deep throat with the best of them but can't drop that fine ass to the floor?" He quirks a brow, then does a jig that looks like some new type of TikTok dance trend.

"Fine," I jump up. A smile spreads across my face. "You're on," I say, letting the light-hearted moment fill me with a new feeling this weekend—freedom. Unrestrained, non-judgmental freedom.

First Time

Luther enters the room as Jones spins me into a dip. He swoops me around, giving me an upside-down view of a scantily clad Luther before pulling me upright. There are leather straps across his chest and shoulders. Tight black briefs cover his lower body.

"What's going on here?" Luther says, sitting down to watch us.

"We're dancing," Jones says, "Drink?"

"Always," Luther says, motioning me forward.

Jones gives me a pat on the butt, pushing me forward in silent approval to approach Luther.

I do.

"Where's Monica?" I ask.

"I left her in good hands," Luther says.

I straddle his lap, still swaying my hips to the music. Luther gently places his hands on my bare hips, letting me lead. I rub myself against his cock. He's not hard yet, but I plan to get him there.

"More for me then," I say boldly. The friction from his clothing feels good against my body, so I rub harder as I swivel my hips.

His dark, deep chuckle tickles the air. "It's all for you, pretty girl." Luther pulls me forward, planting his lips on my neck. He sucks in my skin, hard enough to bruise and light enough to make me want more.

The sway of my body becomes tighter, moving circles around his growing erection. The entire interaction feels so normal. It's at odds with everything we've been doing this weekend, but I still find it sensually intriguing.

Jones sits down beside Luther, handing him a drink. Luther takes a long drink of the cold beverage before pressing his lips to my neck again.

The cold touch of his lips sends shivers down my spine. He pulls back for another drink, capturing an ice cube between his teeth. I extend my neck, inviting him back as goosebumps of anticipation rise on my skin. But Luther stretches me back, palming my breasts.

He pinches my nipple and rubs the ice cube across it, making it go achingly hard. A whimper escapes my lips as cold water slides down my waist, but Jones is kissing me before the sound becomes audible.

The two men are on me, moving me into a new position on the couch. Their mouths claim me, explore me, and pleasure me in a way that is soft and caring—something I didn't think they were capable of until now.

Hell, I hadn't kissed Jones until this very moment. It's weird how well our mouths connect with this being our first time.

Their hands massage my aching muscles. I reach for them, wanting to provide the same pleasure, but a quick hand snatches mine, binding them above my head.

Jones and Luther hover over me. Jones at my mouth, Luther at my waist. They haven't touched that budding ache between my legs, but nevertheless, I'm thirsting for it with insatiable need. I'm exactly where they want me.

"How is this, Kitten?" Jones murmurs against my collarbone.

"Good," I say, arching my back as Luther presses a wet kiss to the inside of my thigh.

Jones keeps my hands bound but uses the other to stroke my breast, kneading and pinching the nipple. "Luther, how wet is she?"

"Let me see," Luther says, his voice muffled between my legs. His hot breath skims my sex, and I clench.

As my body releases, wetness spills out of me. "Oh god," I say as my cheeks heat. These men have seen me in various positions of debauchery all weekend, yet the simple act of my desire being on full display is embarrassing me. It's such a simple, erotic thing for a man to bear witness.

"She's soaked," Luther says. Then his mouth is on me, drinking every last bit of my arousal.

I moan loudly, but Jones is there to capture my sounds of pleasure again. Luther's tongue pushes against my sex, plunging in and out of me. "She's delicious," he says.

As Luther eats me out, Jones kisses me with wild abandon. The two men quickly have my head in a daze, losing myself to the feeling of their mouths.

I grind my hips into Luther's face, and he happily obliges, sucking, nipping, licking all of me while Jones forces his tongue between my lips, opening my mouth so wide that our saliva coats half my face.

"Come on Luther's face, Kitten," Jones says, biting my chin playfully.

"I want you inside me, though," I say.

"I'll give her what she wants," Luther says.

His mouth moves to my clit, and his fingers push inside me—in both ends. He pinches his thumb and forefinger together inside me, rubbing his knuckles against the outside of me as he shakes his fist.

"Oh my god," I say, feeling a familiar tension coiling in my core. Jones smirks knowingly, releasing my hands to slide down my body next to Luther.

Luther stops moving his hand and lifts his head. The two men stare at me between my legs. They shift, spreading my legs further apart.

As Luther withdraws his hand, Jones replaces his. Together, they enter me, and I melt.

Luther takes my backside with two fingers, and Jones takes my sex with his. Then, they slide their tongues across my clit together.

I come so hard it squirts out of me, which only spurs them on further. They mouth me like I'm the most delicious thing on Earth.

Their hands synchronize as they thrust into me, hitting my g-spot from both ends, as their mouths suck me in.

My body shakes uncontrollably as the orgasm racks my body. Sweat coats my brow as I fight the overwhelming sensation hurling through me.

I'm not sure when it ends or if it ever does. Wave after wave of euphoria overtakes me.

Double Trouble

When the orgasm subsides, Jones pulls me upright, jerking off his cock. He pushes against my lips, and I open for him. The wide girth of his shaft stretches my mouth, popping my jaw as I take more of him in.

"You suck Daddy's cock so well," Jones says, holding the back of my head. He presses me against him, not allowing me to retreat as the head of his cock chokes me.

It's a subtle reminder of who he is and who I am before he releases me. I cough. Spit drips from my bottom lip as I catch my breath. The look on Jones's face tells me all I need to know. He's only playing along for my benefit.

I like it, though.

I like knowing this sensual, dominant man is restraining himself for my sake. I like the fact that he desires taking control—the veins in his forearms flexing as he holds himself back from fucking me the way he wants—but wants to give me some semblance of normal intimacy.

Even though I didn't ask for it. I want to give him something in return. Because I know he doesn't give this level of power to others. I'm not sure what makes me so lucky, but I won't count my blessings just yet.

"Daddy, please fuck my throat," I say, sticking out my tongue.

Jones fists my hair and jerks my head back. The stinging pain of his hold sends a tingle down my spine.

"Don't tempt me, Kitten. That dirty mouth drives me crazy, and I'm trying to be on my best behavior," he says as he rubs the head of his cock against my tongue.

I suck in the tip, rolling my tongue around the grooved edge of it.

"You can use that dirty mouth on me all day," Luther says, chuckling.

He stands beside Jones, shoulder to shoulder, aligning his shaft with my mouth. I release Jones and open for Luther. Jones keeps a tight hold on my hair as he steers my mouth to the tip of Luther's cock. I repeat my actions, and Luther rewards me with a low groan of approval as my tongue swirls around the bulbous head.

Heat accumulates between my legs as Jones directs me, forcing me to take turns sucking their cocks. Spit trails down my chin and neck, chilling my skin as it cools. While I deep-throat Luther, Jones slaps his cock against my cheek.

"Is your tight little cunt wet and ready for me, Kitten?" Jones says.

I mumble a yes around Luther's shaft, sucking in my cheeks as I slide to the head. With one last swipe of my tongue, I let his cock drop out of my mouth.

"Yes," I say, looking Jones in the eye this time.

He reaches down and slides one finger through my folds. He slips through so easily. His fingers shine brightly with my arousal. They are more lubricated than his cock is from all my sucking. I thirst for this experience in a way I've never thirsted before—like this is the final act, and everything up until now is no comparison.

"You have such a pretty pussy," he says, spreading me apart and taking a long look at my vagina. Jones closes his eyes and inhales deeply.

It undoes me.

"Please, Daddy. Fuck me already," I say.

Jones bites his bottom lip. "I like it when she begs." He swoops me up, spinning and switching our positions so I straddle his lap.

I waste no time in reaching between us to shove his cock inside me. I sink down onto him with urgency, needing to feel him inside me.

It's too fast, making my body strain against his girth, but it feels too damn good to stop. I rock my hips, adjusting to his size, as the rotation allows me to lubricate him and take him deeper.

He drives his hips up, shoving the remaining length of himself into me. A shallow gasp escapes me as my body holds tightly around him.

"So ready," Jones says, pushing his index finger into my mouth.

I suck on his finger as I bounce on his cock. The tightness is overwhelming, but I fight it.

Jones pulls his finger away from my lips with a pop and reaches around my backside. He pulls my buttcheeks apart as he shoves his finger into my ass. The quick insertion catches me off guard, sending my nerve endings into overdrive and forcing me to halt. Jones takes the lead, fucking up into my pussy as his finger thrusts into me from behind.

He doesn't give me time to overthink anything. An orgasm is already building. That familiar tingling sensation and tightening in my core forces me to fall against Jones's chest.

"Not yet," he says, pulling his finger out of my backside and wrapping an arm around my waist so that I cannot move.

Luther whispers in my ear, "Relax, pretty girl."

The sound of squirting and the cold lube on Luther's cock nudging against my backside is my only warning of what comes next.

Jones holds me tightly as Luther slowly enters my ass. The head of his cock stretches my sphincter. When he pushes past it, all my barriers and restraints are gone. The feeling of his cock going deeper and deeper into my backside has me melting into Jones's chest.

I'm entirely at their mercy now.

And then Jones is moving.

They take it slow, fucking me shallowly, not pulling out very far, as I adjust to the feeling of two men inside me. I'm not sure what to feel other than overwhelmed. My body clenches in one area and then the next as they take turns thrusting.

Jones's lips find my neck, kissing me forcefully, painfully. He nips my jugular, and it's like a bolt of lightning strikes my clit. I cry out, but he doesn't stop.

"Daddy," I say, protesting. Yet, I don't want him to stop.

"Come for us, Kitten," he says against my neck.

At the same time, he and Luther transition. They slam into me at the same time. Their cocks plunge into me, bumping against my G-spot from both ends. Luther pulls me against his chest, forcing my body to take them at a new angle. His mouth finds my ear, and I fully combust.

Final Rapture

"**K**eep going, Kitten," Jones says.

My head spins.

The orgasm barrels through me, not allowing me any semblance of control whatsoever as it rolls through every muscle, tendon, and nerve in my body.

The men keep pounding into me, making wave after wave of ecstasy course through me as I go slack between them. Their hands hold me tightly, perfectly in control as I lose control.

"Let's switch," Jones says.

"Move her to the bed," Luther answers, helping me stand.

I sway, but Jones assists me to the bed as Luther cleans his cock. Jones runs a hand up my backside, circling my hole with his finger while Luther lays down on the bed.

"Climb on top of him," Jones says.

"Okay, Daddy," I answer.

"That's a good girl."

He smacks my ass as I crawl over Luther, positing his head at my center. He slips into me, but we both still moan when he's settled fully inside.

"She's so tight and warm. I could wear this woman out, Jones," Luther says.

Jones pushes my upper back down and says, "I fully plan on exhausting her tonight." He spreads my butt cheeks.

I turn my head to watch him as Luther slowly fucks me. Jones nudges against my backside, slipping in just a fraction of his head before pulling away. He teases me—sticking himself in, then retreating.

"Daddy, please," I say. I don't care how much it hurts. The pleasure outweighs the pain.

"He's admiring the view, pretty girl," Luther says, pulling my face toward him. His lips capture mine, holding me in place, sensually kissing me as slowly as he moves inside me.

Jones takes the opportunity to continue his taunt. Pushing in, then pulling out. Never giving me all of him. All of them.

My asshole greedily holds onto him each time he gives me a taste. The muscles ache when he retracts.

Luther keeps me distracted with his achingly slow pace, feeding that thirsty part of my body just enough to restrain me from screaming for more.

"My turn," Jones says, then fully thrusts himself into me.

My backside is clenched, having waited too long for entrance, forcing him to take me aggressively. But that's how I like it.

When Jones is in me, Luther pulls out. He lets his shaft sit against my clit, leaving my pussy aching to be filled as Jones fucks my ass.

"No, please," I say against Luther's lips.

He chuckles, nipping my bottom lip. "Listen to her beg for it, Jones. Her thirsty little cunt wants both of us," Luther says.

Jones's fingers dig into my hips as he takes me with a brisk thrust. "Taking us both in her pussy will have to wait until next time. Give her one more. Then come in her thirsty little cunt. Give her what she wants."

"My pleasure," Luther says with a growl. He adjusts himself, then enters me.

Again, they take me in turns. It's all so overwhelming. I can't decipher one cock or hole from the other.

All I feel is the smooth grooves of a cock stroking the inner walls of my body. All I smell is a musky, entirely male scent mixing with my heady arousal.

Luther pulls me into another kiss. This time, it's rough and claiming. He opens my mouth, forcing the air from my lungs as his tongue swoops in, demanding I give back. So I do.

I rock my body against theirs, begging them to take me harder. And they do.

My hips fervently shift back, desperate to take the men deeper into me, basking in the glow of taking control despite my vulnerable position between them. Their hands appreciate me, needing the curves on the outside of my body as their cocks do everything else inside.

"Come with me, pretty girl," Luther says, releasing my mouth and taking my neck.

He sucks me in, moaning against my skin as his cock hardens and releases. The heat from his cum fills me, his thrusts become frantic and unrestrained, and I lose myself too. My body tightens, every muscle going frigid before it expels with a whoosh.

Luther bites into my neck, eliciting pain to heighten my pleasure. The mixture of pain and pleasure is a sin. It's far too good a pairing to be anything but the most egregious desire.

When his orgasm fades, Luther pulls out of me and releases my neck. Jones hauls me upright, still seated in my ass. His forearm traps my waist against his chest.

"My turn," he says.

He pulls out of me and shoves into my cunt. The sudden ingress makes my body shudder. The prior orgasm is still on the horizon and threatening to come back with full force. Jones only heightens it as he exploits me—going from my pussy to my ass.

I know it's wrong. It's disgusting. It's unsafe.

But it only makes me relish it more.

"That's it, Kitten. Squeeze me," Jones says, crashing into my pussy.

My body constricts without my control. Jones commands, and I answer.

"Tighter. Don't let me go. I want to feel you," he says. I clench. "Such a good girl."

Jones smooths a hand over my backside, then spanks me. The pain resonates, bringing blood to the sting and heating my lower body.

These men and their ability to coax pleasure from pain and pain from pleasure. I lose myself completely under their hands. Luther joins, capturing my nipple between his teeth. Jones reaches around my body, finding my clit.

"Say my name when you come, Kitten," Jones says.

His forefinger circles my clit. His cock pumps inside me. He swells, kissing my neck as Luther slides a tongue over my nipple and pinches the other.

My body erupts, shaking involuntarily as our orgasms come together.

"Yes, Daddy," I scream.

Jones's arms snuggle me into his chest, his thrusts slow. Our climax reaches its crescendo, then comes down deliciously, warming my chest. It soothes every part of me—mind, body, and soul. It's the release I needed tonight.

The final rapture at the end of an epic weekend.

Afterword

This type of book isn't for everyone, and I completely understand that. It's smut from beginning to end. However, that is the point.

People often ask if I write from experience. I often tell them I write from some experience, some fantasy, and some form of mental hurdle I'm currently battling.

When I wrote Dom Daddy, I was struggling to determine why intimacy was a continuous problem in my previous long-term relationships. The answer is never simple when it involves two people, but when I looked at the part of intimacy only having to do with myself, I discovered what was missing.

I grew up in a religious household in a region of the US known as the Bible Belt. Intimacy, sensuality, and all things that even hinted at sex were something to be kept behind closed doors like it didn't exist. I remember being sent home from school numerous times for wearing shorts or a dress that was too short.

They said that I was drawing attention by showing too much skin—like I didn't show more skin lifeguarding in the summer around all the same people. Truthfully, I was just skinny and tall. Someone a few inches shorter could wear the same thing to school and not be noticed by the skirt police.

But when I did, I was chastised for doing so, and the adult sexualizing my body was seen as a righteous rule follower, guarding young men from having sacrilegious thoughts. They didn't even consider women might be having those same thoughts back then. That would have been too blasphemous to consider in my small town (think Footloose).

Regardless, many things contributed to suppressing my urges and my desires. I blame my childhood for much of it. But as an adult, I had the power to change these thought processes. And so I did.

Dom Daddy is about this awakening. Lily is in much the same position—sexually frustrated and fearing judgment. She takes a leap of faith to explore something casual with a man she meets online, hoping that without judgment, she can figure out why she's so frustrated.

Along the way, she discovers it's not about the lack of sex that makes her so pent up. It's the quality, the connection, the exploration, the freedom, the control, and more. There's a complicated world out there that she is only just discovering.

We're encouraged to explore boundaries in communication and expand our knowledge in business, but why should we not also be encouraged to see what satisfies us physically? Intimacy—both physical and emotional—is something I was forced to learn on my own as an adult. I was never given advice or books to explain my feelings and desires.

For Lily, she starts out as a beginner, testing the waters and happy to let Jones take the lead. Near the end of the book, we discover Jones suspects she has her own path to pave. He doesn't want to suppress her urges like she has already done her entire life. He wants to foster them and help her grow because her journey is not over; it has just begun. By the end, Lily feels more powerful and more comfortable in her own skin than she ever did before.

While not everyone needs to be tied up and whipped to see the light and know what they enjoy physically and emotionally, this is Lily's path. Plus, I think it makes for a fun book.

XOXO
Sam

About the Author

Sam Marie is a contemporary fiction author who loves writing everything from spicy romances to science fiction. When she's not reading or writing, she walks her fur child along the beach, hosts dinner parties, and travels often.

Her love of storytelling started at a young age. Sam often entertained her family on road trips with long-winded stories about wild adventures in make-believe lands, and her love affair with writing only grew from there. She wrote her debut novel, Foreign Desires, in one month, publishing it on a popular online reading platform, Inkitt, as she completed chapters. The community engagement surrounding her stories led Sam to leave the corporate life behind and pursue her passion for writing full-time.

Sign up for her newsletter to stay current on Sam's book news. You can also follow her here:

Website: authorsammarie.com

Facebook: Sam Marie

Instagram: @author.sam.marie

Tiktok: @sammarieofficial

Linktree: linktr.ee/sammarie.author

Goodreads: Sam Marie

Sam's Titles

Find all of Sam's titles and the latest information on upcoming releases here: